{a novel by}

KACHI UGO

MEWRANTERS

ATTACK OF THE SEA MONSTER

NEW YORK

LONDON • NASHVILLE • MELBOURNE • VANCOUVER

Mewranters

Published in New York, New York, by Morgan James Publishing. Morgan James is a trademark of Morgan James, LLC.
www.MorganJamesPublishing.com

The Morgan James Speakers Group can bring authors to your live event. For more information or to book an event visit The Morgan James Speakers Group at www.TheMorganJamesSpeakersGroup.com.

Publisher's Note: This novel is a work of fiction. Names, characters, places, and incidents are either products of the author's imagination or used fictitiously. All characters are fictional, and any similarity to people living or dead is purely coincidental.

ISBN 978-1-64279-075-7 paperback
ISBN 978-1-64279-076-4 case laminate
ISBN 978-1-64279-077-1 eBook
Library of Congress Control Number: 2018942770

Cover Illustration and Cover & Interior Design by:
Megan Whitney Dillon
Creative Ninja Designs
megan@creativeninjadesigns.com

In an effort to support local communities, raise awareness and funds, Morgan James Publishing donates a percentage of all book sales for the life of each book to Habitat for Humanity Peninsula and Greater Williamsburg.

Get involved today! Visit
www.MorganJamesBuilds.com

To Mom and Dad, for keeping me inspired,
to Pastor Gee, for your prayers and words of encouragement,
and to Lt. Col. Moyo Akin-Ojo, who kept me writing
when all I wanted to do was stop.

CONTENTS

1

THE FALL RITUAL

Perry Johnson awoke with a feeling of dread. He knew his time had come, and he felt he was going to fail. He had never been good at anything. Not sports, not hanging out with friends, not even school. He wasn't failing in school, but he wasn't passing either. He was average. In everything. Nothing special. That kind of sucked. But what could he do? It was who he was. It was his destiny.

Even as he sat trembling on his bed, he figured today was going to end badly. Badly for him. He was certain he wasn't going to be good enough. He had known about the ritual for some time since Richard. He was four then. One week after they had celebrated Richard's twelfth birthday, the family moved to their cliff house in Nevada. Perry didn't know what Richard did because he wasn't allowed to watch, but whatever Richard had done, he had been awesome. Four years later, Jane and Jake's turn came. He didn't watch, again, but he knew they were great. Now his time had come. One week after they had celebrated his twelfth birthday, they had moved here. It was his turn, but Perry already knew what the outcome would be.

Perry knew he wasn't good enough. Whatever this family ritual was, he was going to fail it. Perry had always gotten by being average. Somehow, he suspected that this time average wouldn't be good enough. That's why he was afraid. The ritual was important—like family-tradition important. That much he knew. He loved his sister so much. He couldn't bear the thought of losing her, but that didn't stop these thoughts from barraging his mind. Average meant failure, and failure was his one-way ticket out of the family.

"Perry!" His mother's voice came to him from somewhere in the cabin. "Breakfast is ready."

Perry had already gotten used to his small room. Still, it pressed in on him from all sides. He had no appetite for food. Yet, he knew he must eat. It might very well be his last meal as Perry, son of Johnson.

Perry jumped off the bed. He landed on the floorboards with a crouch, his legs almost giving in. He had on a red shirt and blue jeans. He looked in the mirror on his dresser. All he saw was a small, scrawny preteen. He gulped. His heart was already pounding, though he kept his breathing steady.

The door to his room opened. Lisa, his dear sister, came in. She had a warm smile on her face and a small broom in her hands.

"Mother told me to do your chores," Lisa said, mild irritation on her face.

"She did?" Now his breathing became erratic. "Why?"

Lisa frowned at the way he breathed. She shrugged and said, "Don't know. Something about a big day for you. I heard her talking with Richard."

Perry struggled to calm himself. He swallowed hard. "Richie's here?"

"Mmm-Hmm," Lisa replied, already sweeping the floor. She was eleven years old. Perry might not be here to watch her do the ritual next year, but he knew she would excel. She was unlike him. Success came naturally to her, the same way being average came naturally to him. It was who they were. Maybe, if he could get his parents to understand this, they wouldn't kick him out of the family when he botched the family ritual.

Spurred by impulse and a humongous amount of nervous energy, Perry hugged his sister and left the room. He could never hate his sister. Not even when his parents praised her and derided him. He couldn't even be jealous of her.

Perry walked the narrow corridor, which opened to the small sitting room. His heart lurched. Richard, Jane, and Jake were all present. Richard sat at the table with Jake, while Jane sat on a couch. Mother wasn't in the room. But there was food on the table, which Richard and Jake ate. There was an extra plate; his, Perry concluded. He hesitated in the low-light corridor. Usually, when Richard came from Maine, or Jake and Jane, their family's inseparable twins, came from school in California, Perry felt exuberant. But now he could feel his heart sink. He didn't want them to see him fail. He didn't want to eat, but he knew he must.

A hand touched his shoulder, and he jerked away, frightened. He was in the sitting room now, in the open, exposed. At first, he was startled. Everyone seemed happy to see him. He felt like a spotlight was upon him. Richard, Jake, and Jane talked excitedly, all at the same time, but he couldn't pick out their words. All he was conscious of was the ferocity with which his heart hammered in his chest. He looked at where he had been. His mother stood in the doorway, staring at him, concerned. The room fell quiet.

His mother pointed at the table. "Eat," she rumbled.

Perry nodded in submission, sat, and ate. He forced the cheese pie into his mouth, down his throat. Richard watched him, silent, but Jake talked. Talked about the weather. Talked about school. Talked about birds. Richard gave him a sharp look when he mentioned birds, and he quickly changed the topic. Talked about family traditions.

Jake only talked this much when he was antsy. He probably knew Perry's chances of success were thin and feared for him. Perry felt like crying. Why did he have to be such a loser?

Mother roamed the house. She too was nervous. Jane gave nippy glances at him and his food; they flickered from impatience to anxiety. Father wasn't in sight. But he too, no doubt, thought he was no good. Perry fought the urge to wail out in distress and continued battling with his cheese pie and milkshake.

The air seemed to thicken as he pushed it through his lungs. Perry didn't get to the last slice of the crusty cream pie before Father came into the sitting room.

He looked first at Perry. His weathered face carried deep lines on his forehead. In these deep lines, strips of sweat lay. His blue T-shirt had a dark V that reached from his neck. The dark stain was perspiration. Then, his gaze shifted to Mother. "They are ready for him," he said in a solemn tone.

It was as if a giant bell rang in Perry's mind. He knew he was finished. Why remain there? He jumped out of his chair and was about to run for his room. But his mother stood, akimbo, in his path, with a look of concern on her face. She didn't seem to have noticed his intentions. He squashed the urge to run and kept hidden those intentions.

Richard, Jake, and Jane rose to their feet, a sudden reverence around their motions. They stood still, allowing Mother to guide him towards the door with one hand on his shoulder. Father gave way, and Perry walked into the hot desert.

Three strange-looking men stood by the metal interlocking fence. One was old and the other two were young. But they both looked like they were from an ancient Indian tribe. The old man sported a white shirt, a white headband, and a white feather sticking up by his left ear. His intense gaze drilled holes into Perry's eyes. Perry looked away. Beyond the fence, less than ten feet away, was an edge. Father had told him that the edge was fifty stories above the desert floor. Father had also told him that anyone who fell off the cliff would splatter into a million bloody pieces.

Mother's grip tightened on Perry's shoulder. She pushed him gently towards the strange men. Father and the rest followed from behind.

As Perry glanced around the yard, he realized there was only one car beside the house. How had these men, including Richard and the twins, gotten to the cabin? There wasn't a highway for miles. What was going on?

Perry caught the look in Mother's side glances to Father. She was uncertain. Unsure. Like she knew this was his last day as her son. But, she couldn't call off the ritual now that these strange men were involved.

When they were still a distance from the three men, they halted. His mother crouched beside him, held his shoulders with both hands, and fixed him with her most dangerous stare. Whatever she said now, he could never disobey; not if he didn't want to suffer severe consequences.

"Those men are here to test you," his mother said with a brief glance at the old man. "He's the chief of our clan. Do whatever he tells you, and it will be all right. Fail, and you might lose that which is precious to you."

Perry's dread heightened. *Lose Lisa?*

"Mother?" Perry croaked. "I'm scared."

His mother's fierce gaze melted that instant. She looked at his heaving chest for a moment. Then she turned to face his father. Her knees gave out beneath her.

"He's not ready," she muttered to him, tears in her eyes.

Father picked up Mother from the ground and held her in his arms. "There's nothing we can do about that," he whispered back to her. "It's either now or never."

"What if he fails?" Mother said, glancing at Perry, who now stood alone.

His father's eyes gripped his. "Then it's over for him." He said this without an iota of emotion.

Mother squeezed her eyes shut as tears fell to her cheek. When she opened her eyes, she fixed a cold stare on him. "Do as I say."

Perry turned away from his family. The three strange men remained passive and silent as he approached them. The sun scorched his head. Baked sand found its way into his jeans. He looked over his shoulder one last time. Mother and Father weren't looking. They were locked in an embrace. Richard and the twins were farther behind, staring at him with glassy eyes, squinting in the sun. The house stood behind them, the only human structure for as far as the eyes could see. It was small, misshapen, a construction of roofing sheets. It had been his family's cabin for years, since before he was born. He was about to lose it. He was about to lose everything.

"Perry Johnson," the old man said. His voice was unusually strong considering his age; he had wrinkles all over his face.

Perry stood before the man. "Yes, Sir," he replied, looking up at the man, into the sun.

The man placed a hand on his shoulder and led him towards the gate in the fence. "Do you know what this is all about, Perry?" he asked.

Perry shook his head, too scared to talk.

The man made a sound, an amusing sound. "Surely, you must have an inkling as to what purpose you have been brought here."

"A family ritual." Perry's voice was lost in the wind, but the man must have heard because he nodded contemplatively.

"Go on," he said. They were through the gate and headed for the edge of the cliff.

"A test to determine if I'm worthy to be a member of this family," Perry said. A sudden alarm came to his mind as they approached the edge. The desert floor spread from underneath the cliff: a barren, dry land. Great winds moved sand around in disorganized sweeps. "Sir, why are we going towards the edge of the cliff?"

"Does it bother you?"

"It's dangerous, Sir. My father has forbidden me to cross the fence," Perry said, trying to look over his shoulder at his parents. But, the old man prevented him. Perry tried to wriggle himself out of the man's grip, but the man clamped tighter.

"Not to birds, it's not," the old man said, pausing at the very edge of the cliff.

Perry felt queasy standing fifty stories above the ground. He shut his eyes and craned his neck away from the fall. "I'm not a bird, Sir," he cried out in desperation.

"Not yet," the man said, and shoved him over the cliff.

Perry fell.

Fell towards his death.

He hurtled.

Hurtled to splatter into a million bloody pieces.

He screamed, flapped, and beat the air. But, he fell on. The floor—his death—rushed up to meet him. His heart fluttered ferociously. A flame of fear erupted around his body. Ten seconds to his death. A strange feeling came over him, unlike his earlier feeling of apprehension. Feathers sprung from his skin. His legs turned to talons. A different kind of fear overtook his mind. More feathers shot out of his skin.

Five seconds to his death.

Perry flapped his hands faster, as if he could fly. The wind caught on his hands—no—his wings! He flapped again and glided away from the cliff wall. He was no longer falling. He was gliding, two yards above the ground! He cried out, terrified, but what came forth from his sharp beak was a piercing whistle that rang through the desert.

He tried to grab the sand before crashing into the ground. He tried to push his body off the sand with his hands, but they weren't strong enough because they were wings. Panic stabbed at Perry's heart. He flapped off the ground, rising five feet into the air. The sand lodged in his skin felt like tiny pinpricks, irritating him. He landed on talons, shaking his body vigorously.

I can't be a bird! he thought. *I CAN'T BE A BIRD!*

Wait, maybe I succeeded this time! Did I pass the test?!

He looked to the cliff. It was so far away. Yet he could clearly see his parents, Richard, the twins, and the three strange men. He searched their faces for recognition or approval, but it was not happy surprise or awe that he saw. It was terror. His heart sank. He was a failure again. What else was new?

Before his eyes, they turned into huge birds. Huger than normal birds, but not different in other regards. Mother was a white owl. Father was a blue harrier. Richard was a grey hawk. The twins were bright yellow buzzards. The old man that had tried to kill him was a white osprey. Perry blinked, not sure what he was seeing. They soared high above the desert towards him.

When they got to him, they circled, keeping their distance.

He glanced down at his own body. He was a golden eagle. He spread his wings and they each stretched over a yard from his chest. The circling birds scampered away at the revelation of his full form, seemingly terrified. Perry nestled his wings back into his body and sat on the ground, dropping his head. He felt ashamed of being an eagle. He had failed his parents, his family. He had broken his family's tradition. He deserved to be expelled from the fold.

After a while, he heard his mother speak. Her voice was firm in his mind. *"Perry, rise into the air. We're going to teach you to handle your aerial form."*

Even though he heard her voice in his mind, he knew it was a command, not a request. He leaped into the air, spreading his wings full length. The air seemed to cling to his form, pushing him upwards. He didn't need to flap. He shot to the clouds, his shame melting into excitement. His family and the osprey followed behind, instructing him.

2

THE FAMILY SECRET

P erry trained all day.

At first, he was terrified that he would remain a bird forever, but when his parents assured him that he could change back and forth between human and eagle, all he wanted to do was fly. He was stronger, faster, more agile than the others. He felt like he owned the sky. He felt like the winds were his birthright, his subjects. He was taught the basics of flight, but he knew he was infinitely capable of much more.

When Perry was able to handle his aerial form better, he raced across the desert. He stretched his wings as far as they would go, he stretched his tail as far as it would go, and he pierced through the air like a dart headed home. The air streamed around his body, pulling him deeper. His mother had forbidden him to fly too high, so he flew low. His huge form shadowed the sandy desert floor, and he left waves of sandstorm in his wake.

His parents, Richard, and the osprey followed from behind, giving him bits and pieces of information on flying here and there. But, the buzzard twins tried to match his speed. They only succeeded in lagging behind him, and he wasn't even pushing his full strength. For once in his life, Perry didn't feel like a loser. He didn't feel average. He owned the skies. He was master of the winds. They did his bidding. Perry rolled, twisted, and pulled stunts that amazed his brothers.

As dusk neared, Perry learned about communication. There were several levels of communication amongst their kind. Each level was esoteric and could only be assessed by relationship or bond. He could hear his parents and siblings because they were family. He could hear the clan chief because he was clan. No one outside the family would be able to listen in on their communication because they weren't family and they weren't clan. He was cautioned about the relationships he entered with people. He could bring harm to his family and to the clan if he formed a bond with the wrong kind of person.

It was dark when his flight training ended for the day.

Changing back was easy, so said his brother, Richard. All he had to do was approach the ground, see—*imagine*, Mother had corrected—himself walking on the ground—not landing—and his powers would do the rest. They had all turned back to humans except him. He had crashed into the ground eighteen times before he got it right. And when he did, he came off the ground with bruises.

They sat around a fire, which had been built by one of the two young men who came with the clan chief. The other man was inside the house, ensuring that Lisa wasn't watching. If she knew the details of the Fall Ritual, it could lead to "problems" when her turn finally came.

They were silent at first as Mother tended to his bruises. Her hands trembled on his skin. Perry looked around. He remembered the terror in their faces earlier in the day. Strangely, he could not only see it in their faces but feel it. It was as if his perceptiveness had multiplied hundredfold. They were all scared, and he could tell that he was the object of their fear. The clan chief showed no sign of fear, but it was as if Perry could hear his heart race.

Perry's excitement crashed into a million bloody pieces. He knew it was too good to be true, that they should all be impressed with his performance. There was no moon up in the sky; there was no wind in the air. The fire spit and crackled. Mother finished cleaning his wounds and sat beside him.

The chief closed his eyes for a moment, seemingly enjoying the pop of the fire, almost bobbing his head to it. He drew in a deep breath. "Perry," he said in a sage-like tone, "do you know what happened to you today?"

Pictures of his eagle form swamped Perry's mind. The urge came over him to run for the cliff and soar into the night. The excitement tingled, but he reined it in. Maybe when they all went to bed, he would indulge himself. "I transformed into a huge golden eagle," he said, the excitement not lost in his voice.

Richard cast a fearful glance at their father, then at the chief. Father looked at the clan chief, apprehensive, like Perry had broken a sacred code or something and Father was now wondering if the chief would punish his son. The chief didn't seem to notice their stares.

The chief merely smiled, bobbing his head to the music from the fire. "A huge golden eagle it is, boy," the chief said.

His mother let out a short gasp of terror.

The chief didn't seem to notice that either. "Do you know what we are?" he asked.

Perry didn't know if it was because of the family bond, or if it was strictly an eagle thing, but he could feel his mother tremble with fear. Profound fear. Like she was afraid for her life, or his life. What had he done wrong?

"No, Sir," Perry replied the clan chief, sullen once more.

"We call ourselves Mewranters," the chief said. He closed his eyes again, bobbing his head to the sizzle and crackle of the fire. "Mews have existed since the dawn of time. Since the beginning of evil. We are like a force for good, preventing evil from growing rampant in the world."

"Like cops?" Perry chirped in, his exhilaration building despite the glum surrounding his family.

The chief smiled but he did not open his eyes. "Yes. Like cops. But our work is...different. We are nature's police."

"Tell me, Perry, do you think dragons and monsters exist?" The chief opened his eyes. They were devoid of any expression.

Perry shook his head. "Dragons and monsters aren't real. They are simply a figment of our imagination."

The chief nodded, thoughtful. Then, his face turned dark. "But you see," he said with an ominous tone, "they are very real. Dragons, beastly creatures of the night, monsters—they are all real."

Perry frowned, resisting the chill that was settling on him. "But I've only seen them on TV and in books. They aren't real."

"You think they aren't real because we do a very good job," the chief replied. "If there are no sea monsters ravaging the seven seas, or three-headed hydras prowling the streets, it's not because they don't exist. It's because *we* exist. We are the last line of defense against nature's indiscretions. We are nature's police. We are Mewranters."

"Nature's police?"

"Look at it this way, Perry," Richard said. "Nature has two forms: the good form and the bad. The good form is the reason for all the normal animals, insects, and so on. The bad form is the reason for monsters. The good form is the dominant form of nature, but the bad form finds expression now and then. We, *Mewranters*, are empowered to keep evil nature at bay for the good of all mankind."

"Nature has an evil twin sister?"

Richard chuckled. "Yes. You could say that."

"Our existence," the chief continued, "is a secret to the world, and it must remain that way. Do you understand? You cannot reveal your true identity to anyone, not even your closest friends. That means you cannot change before human eyes. It must always be done in secret."

Perry nodded. He wasn't about to tell anyone he could change into a bird. They'd laugh at him.

The chief relaxed a bit and nodded to the tune of the fire. "Now, a Mew can naturally transform into three forms. An aerial form, a terrestrial form, and an aquatic form. This enables him to do his work in all the spheres of the world: the sea, the land, and the air. Each transformation would put him at the top of the food chain; larger than other natural forms. For example, every Mew transforms into a bird of prey. And a Mew bird of prey is at least three times the size of a natural bird of prey. As for terrestrial forms, every Mew transforms into a predator."

"When do I get to change into my terrestrial form?"

"Not until your thirteenth birthday, Son," the chief replied. "Then, the aquatic form erupts when you're fourteen. That's the order."

"Why is the aerial form first?"

"Because birds represent the highest form of evolution," the chief replied. "A Mew starts his journey from the top and works his way to the bottom."

"I understand," Perry said.

"Good. Every Mew belongs to a clan. Every clan has a clan chief and a leadership structure. I am the clan chief of your family's clan and therefore your clan. There are forty-six Mew clans spread across continental America and hundreds more all over the world." The clan chief paused before continuing. "You must remember this, Perry; not every Mew is on your side. Just because we fight the same enemy doesn't mean we are friends. I'm afraid the expression, 'the enemy of my enemy is my friend,' doesn't apply to Mews. There have been wars in the past. Deaths." The clan chief's gaze shifted to his mother. "Parents have lost children. Loved ones."

There was silence.

Perry could feel his mother's grief pour out of her like a river. Who had she lost because of a clan war?

"Your clan is your blood. When you swear the oath of a Mew, you'll also be swearing allegiance to this clan. Every clan has its own territory. As long as your Mew activities are restricted to our territory, the state of New York, you should have no problem with other Mews."

The clan chief continued his lecture on his family's secret, but Perry had already zoned out. His mother's grief was strong. Aside from that, he could not shake off the feeling that something was wrong. Everyone kept sneaking glances at him. And when he caught them, all he saw was apprehension. The chief said something about rules for transformation and issued a strong warning about staying away from a certain mansion on a certain street in Brooklyn, but Perry wasn't listening. He and his mother had locked gazes.

Perry searched his mother's eyes for an answer to their strange behaviors and found none. He felt depressed. He could never be good enough for his parents or his clan. Not even when he was an eagle.

"Perry Johnson," the clan chief rumbled, "do you, this day, swear to fulfill your duties as a Mew until your very last breath?"

Perry glanced at his father. He nodded his approval.

"I do," Perry said, solemn.

"Do you swear allegiance to the clan of your father and his father before him?"

"I do."

"Then, by the power vested in me as the clan chief, I hereby accept you as a member of the Sherwood Clan."

Silence followed the clan chief's proclamation.

Perry didn't feel different. There were no fireworks, no spectacular occurrences to demonstrate that the clan chief's words held any real power. All he felt was a ton of weight on his heart. He just wanted to go to bed and forget about today. Return to being average and unspectacular.

"It's done," the chief said. "He's one of us now."

The young man, who had been sitting quietly beside the chief, spoke for the first time. "Then we must prepare for war," he said, "because the other clans will come for him."

"Not here, Pane," the chief retorted harshly.

A loud cawing sound came to them from the high north. Perry looked. A bird. A Mew-sized vulture gliding lazily in their direction. No one saw the creature at first except him. The black vulture circled in the dark clouds for a while. Scanning for trouble. Seeing none, it descended upon the gathering, swooping in from the cliff end. Less than a yard to the dusty desert floor, the vulture changed into a tall, slender man. His feet kissed the ground, neither stopping nor breaking in stride. It was a perfect and seamless transformation.

The man had long black hair. He strode towards the gathering, his black overcoat flailing behind him.

"What's he doing here?" Mother whispered to the chief, her voice betraying her fear. "Do you think they know about him?"

Perry shuddered with dread. *What about him?*

The chief shook his head—an almost imperceptible gesture. "It's too soon. They can't know about Perry." The chief then locked gaze with the man, smiled, and said, "Welcome Mr. Monte, Messenger of the Council. What message have you brought us?"

3

MR. MONTE, THE MESSENGER VULTURE

The man stood still in the light, gazing from one person to another. He paused at Perry for a while. "Is that the initiate?" he said, pointing at Perry. He had a mysterious look in his eyes.

"Yes," Father replied.

"What form did he take?"

A sudden tightness filled the air.

Silence.

The man's eyes contracted, and a hint of amusement slid the side of his lips. He looked to the clan chief. The clan chief returned his gaze.

"What form did he take?" he said in a measured but authoritative voice.

The clan chief drew a long breath, let it out, and asked again, "What message have you brought us?"

This stunned Mr. Monte. He gazed at the chief for a full minute in silence. His whole black outfit bristled with wounded pride.

"It doesn't matter if you answer the question here or at the Council meeting. You will have to answer it. You have been summoned."

Fear rippled across the gathering.

Mother, Father, and Richard exchanged clipped but dreadful glances.

"Why?" the chief asked.

Mr. Monte briefly glanced at Perry. "Not before the initiate."

"He's now one of us," the chief said, sweeping his hand to Perry's side. "Better he learns about the Council and their powers now than later."

Mr. Monte gave the chief another long gaze, one that prickled with anger. It seemed that the chief was breaking a code or protocol. Whatever the case, Mr. Monte didn't like it. But, he couldn't do a thing about it. After all, he was just a messenger. His task was to deliver a message and be gone. He had no say. He wasn't seen often, and he had little power. He was average, just like Perry. Only in Mr. Monte's case, he served a good purpose. Perry didn't. All Perry seemed to be able to do was get into trouble and cause his parents' heartache, just like he had done by turning into an eagle.

"The sea monster has reawakened," said the messenger.

The reaction was immediate.

Pane jerked to his feet. Mother and Father sat up straight. Richard had a look of abject terror on his face. Even the chief, who could hide his emotions very well, looked shocked.

"Send the boy away," the chief instructed.

Mother grabbed Perry from the stool and led him away from the fire. Halfway to the house, she pushed him in the direction of the door. "Go to bed. And don't come out."

Perry left without turning back. Before he entered the house, he gazed at the skies. Somewhere in the darkness above, Jake and Jane were patrolling in their aerial forms.

Returning to the living room, his heart hammered in his chest. Lying on the couch was the figure of a man. He was asleep. Lisa wasn't in the sitting room. Perry figured she was asleep, too.

Perry paced in the dark. He couldn't bring himself to calm down. The sea monster had reawakened. That was a very, *very* bad thing. Perry crouched near the window, pulled away the curtain drapes so he could see the fire. Mother paced at the side, her hands on her waist. The buzzard twins were there, now in human form. Mr. Monte sat down beside the chief and looked into the fire. Father was occluded by Richard whose face still projected great fear. Though far away, Perry could still sense the tightness hanging in the air.

Mr. Monte began to talk. To Perry's surprise, he heard every word as if he were right there beside him.

"The sea monster reawakened earlier today," the messenger said. "In the morning, to be precise."

"Where is it?" Mother stopped to ask.

"The whole eastern seaboard. But mostly around New York. It seems to have picked a home there."

Mother gave a high-pitched sigh and paced on.

"Any casualties?"

Mr. Monte shrugged. "I don't know. I was sent to you the moment it became clear that the monster was alive. However, if the rumors are anything to go by, I'd say seven Mews are already dead."

"Seven?" The shock was evident in Pane's voice.

Mr. Monte ignored him and looked at the clan chief who gazed at the fire, though this time his eyes swarm with intensity. "You have been summoned, Chief of Sherwood Clan." Mr. Monte stood to leave.

The clan chief looked up at him. "Wait. On whose authority?"

"The High Lord himself."

"What does he think is the cause of the reawakening? What do *they* think is the cause?"

Mr. Monte smiled. "I think you already know the answer to that."

"Is it only our clan chief who is summoned?" This came from Father.

"No," Mr. Monte replied. "All the clan chiefs across the States have been summoned to the American Heartland for an emergency meeting. Whatever the true cause of the sea monster's reawakening, we shall find out there."

Mother stopped short and shot Father a deadly look. Then she glanced at the chief.

Mr. Monte made to leave, but stopped. He turned and said, "There have been talks... That the cause of this reawakening is the same as the previous."

"What nonsense is that?!" Mother replied shrilly. "You think Perry is an eagle? Is that what you think?"

Mr. Monte was silent for a moment, searching Perry's mother's eyes. "I am not saying anything, Mrs. Johnson. But, people out there think an eagle has been born. It won't be long before they remember your son."

Mr. Monte turned away. He took two long strides towards the fence, and then he transformed and ascended into the gloom above.

The chief rose to his feet. "Get Marcus," he said to Pane.

Pane sprinted to the house.

Perry left the curtain, fell to the floor, and crawled to the dining table. He hid there.

Pane opened the door but remained outside. "Marcus. Marcus," he called twice.

"Yeah?" Marcus replied lazily, twirling on the couch.

"We're leaving," Pane said, slamming the door at his last word.

Marcus groaned and twirled for a short while. Then, he got up and left the house.

Perry waited under the table until he counted thirty heartbeats. Breathing elevated, Perry crept on all fours to the window. He rose to a crouch, pulled the drapes apart, and peered out the window. Marcus and Pane were already gone. Perry watched the chief transform into a massive osprey and climb the air.

The moment the white osprey was lost in the darkness above, Mother turned to Father and said, "We have to get him far away from here."

"Far away from where, Joanna?" Father stood to his feet.

"I don't know!" Mother yelled. She laid her hands on her forehead as if she had a headache. "Far away from all this. Where they can't find him."

"And where is that?" Father was angry now. His voice rose a tad louder. "It doesn't matter where we take him! They'll still find him and end him."

Perry's heart was already racing, yet he still felt it climb his chest. *End me?*

"Father is right, Mother," Richard said beside Mother. "If we run away with him, they'll suspect sooner and come for him. Everyone. We can't fight every Mew in the country."

"So what, we just let him go back to school?" Jane asked. "Act like everything is all right? The frigging sea monster is ALIVE. Seven Mews are already dead! Gosh! What are we going to do?!"

"Not panicking would be a good start," Father said, eyeing Jane. He touched Mother. She jerked away at first. He persisted. The second time, she didn't resist.

"This could be a sea monster scare, you know," he said, leading Mother towards the house. The rest followed from behind.

"It's not if seven people are already dead," Joanna said. She wriggled away from Father. "No, not this time. This time it's real. Perry is in danger."

They all fell silent.

The drapes fell off Perry's hands. He scurried out of the sitting room down the short corridor and into his room. He locked the door, slid underneath the bed sheaths, and shut his eyes, sobbing quietly.

He heard the door open and close. He heard someone sit on a chair. He heard everything that was said. They spoke in whispers.

"So, what do we do now?" It was Mother's voice. But, it was different. It was choked with emotions, like she was crying. "Eagle Mews are not safe anywhere in this world. They will come for him. And they will kill him if we go back to New York."

"How would they know? Nobody knows he's an eagle except the chief and his boys," Father replied. "They'll keep the secret to their graves. We'll return to New York and continue with our normal lives. Let the Council handle the sea monster."

"What if he goes looking for trouble?" Jake spoke this time; his voice was cold as ice. "If he transforms into an eagle before other Mews? Word will spread. Shouldn't we tell him the truth?"

"No," Father said. "No one tells Perry anything about the sea monster or the danger he's in. He might do something stupid and get himself killed. So, tell Perry nothing. Agreed?"

They all grumbled their agreement.

"And, if they ask us what Perry turned into," Jane asked, "what do we say then?"

"The same thing the chief will say to the Council. His transformation failed."

"Get some sleep," Father said, a slight cheerfulness in his voice. "This thing will blow over in a matter of days. You'll see."

For a while there were no voices. No movement. Only the sound of his heart beating in his ears. The tears had stopped flowing. Now he was weak, exhausted. Someone began to talk in whispers later, but Perry was far gone in sleep to hear what was said.

4
PERRY GETS A BROWN TRANSOTHE

n the morning, Richard and the twins were gone. According to Father, they left early to catch up with work and school. They were packed and ready to go before sunrise. The house still bristled with apprehension. Unspoken truth was evident in his mother's and father's gazes and movements. Lisa was oblivious to all of this as she sat at the dining table, feasting on the cold meal. Perry had no appetite for food, yet he couldn't disobey his mother. Perry didn't know how he was able to hear their conversation last night, but he was frightened. He never asked to be an eagle Mew. In fact, he wanted to go back to being ordinary. Average.

"Eat your food, honey," his mother said. She looked at him with concern.

Perry had been caught staring into space again.

Lisa frowned at him while munching the stale sandwich.

"Sorry, Mother," Perry said, dropping his eyes from his mother's stare to the sandwich on the plate before him. He had barely touched it. Two bites, no more. He picked it up and forced a portion of the snack into his mouth and bit firmly. His hunger piqued.

Mother and Father sat at the table with them, exchanging restrained glances now and then. They ate quietly in the near darkness. As they were getting ready to leave the old house, strokes of sunlight began to penetrate the room. They packed into the worn station wagon. Father started the vehicle while Mother locked the cabin.

The darkness was lifting from the desert. The air was frigid and dry, and Perry found himself sneezing more often to expel the dust from his nostrils. Through the backseat window, he searched the skies, a building desire in his heart. They were clear, cloudless.

Mother got into the passenger seat, and Father drove off.

Perry now understood how the clan chief, his boys, Richard, and the twins had come to the cabin. *Why drive when you can fly?* He glanced at Lisa. She was engrossed in a red book beside him. He wondered whether all this seemed strange to her.

They were on the highway heading east. Less than an hour after, a wave of sandstorms whipped up. Father was doing one-twenty miles per hour. Mother searched the skies constantly. Perry's life was in danger.

They drove for hours.

Perry tried to sleep, but couldn't. Perry tried to read a book, but couldn't. He couldn't get rid of the tightness in his throat. And, he couldn't get his body to remain still. He felt tormented.

The drive to their cabin house had been fun and lively. But the drive back was dreary. No one talked. Not even Mother and Father. And they never stopped once. They drove until the sun was setting in the west. Then, they had come to Denver, Colorado. They found a roadside motel and rested for the night.

They rented only one room; Mother wanted to keep an eye on him. There were two beds in the room. Lisa stayed on Father's bed while Perry slept on Mother's. Sleep came fast to everyone except Perry. He was troubled. He didn't want to sleep because he didn't want to see the sea monster in his dreams again. Last night had been horrible.

Perry tossed in bed.

If what he had seen was really the sea monster, then all Mews all over the world had a profound reason to be in fear. But why him? Why did he have to dream about the sea monster? What was it about him being an eagle Mew that had reawakened it? And why did he have this unbearable drive to head out to the Atlantic Ocean?

"Perry, are you awake?"

Perry stiffened. He half expected a whack on his head. He shouldn't be awake by this time. "Yes, Mother," he whispered, shutting his eyes and expecting some form of physical rebuke.

"Why?" Surprisingly, there was no retort in her voice. Only concern.

Perry's first urge was to say nothing and get back to pretending to be asleep. But before he could act on the urge, he blurted, "What's the sea monster, Mother?"

Perry felt his mother draw a sharp breath, like she was dealing with an asthmatic attack. She sighed and switched on the lamp. She leaned on her elbow, looking him in the eyes. Her thick black hair fell behind her beautiful face. Joanna wasn't a big woman, but she wasn't a small woman either. Average height, average build, grey eyes, all of which Lisa had inherited.

Mother looked over Perry at Father. He was sleeping with a silent snore; Lisa cozied up in his embrace.

"What do you already know about the sea monster?"

Perry knew a lot of things about the sea monster. Like, he knew that he had caused its reawakening. He knew that it was probably in New York, waiting to kill him. He also knew that there was an emergency meeting currently going on concerning the monster which involved all clan chiefs in America. But, saying all that to his mother would mean he had to give up his secret. The one where he could hear and see as well in human form as he could in eagle form. He didn't know if that was normal for Mews. But if they didn't ask, he wouldn't tell.

"That it has reawakened," Perry said, blinking his eyes like he knew nothing else. It wasn't a lie. It was just an incomplete truth.

His mother nodded thoughtfully. She got off the bed and searched her handbag and took out a small brown cloth. She sat back down on the bed. "The sea monster is a creature of immense power and evil," she said, fiddling with the brown cloth. "It destroys everything and everyone in its path. And it only gets stronger with time. Don't think too much on this, honey. There are powerful Mews in the country that can take care of the creature."

Perry nodded. Of course, he didn't believe her last statement. If it were true, why were they so terrified when they heard of its revival? Perry wanted more information, but he dared not press. He shouldn't even be awake at this time.

His mother handed him the brown cloth. Perry took it in his hands.

"I should have given that to you yesterday," she said. "It's your transo-the, so keep it with you everywhere you go, no matter what."

"Yes, Mother," Perry replied. He was surprised at how soft and pleasing the material felt. There was something else about the material. It made his Mew powers come alive, tingle. Like an adrenaline rush. He wanted to ask his mother what it was, but he was afraid she would think he was taking undue advantage of her magnanimity in letting him be awake at this time.

"Now, Perr, go to sleep," she said, switching off the lamp. "We have a long day today."

Perry held the cloth to his heart. Somehow, it helped him fall asleep faster. However, his dreams of the sea monster were more vivid and frightening.

They were back on the road before sunrise.

Perry still felt groggy, so he found himself slipping in and out of sleep the whole journey. It was a fearful, kaleidoscopic display of buildings, cars, people, the sea, a huge green monster, and a taunting voice. Perry found himself jerking out of sleep with silent gasps that his parents were too busy searching the skies to notice.

"Are you all right? Why do you keep doing that?" Lisa asked, startling him a little. He had forgotten she was there beside him.

Perry gave her a guarded frown, noticing their mother's gaze in his periphery. "I'm fine." He turned away and for a transient moment, he thought he saw a huge red-tailed bird high up the skies—Mew huge. His heart caught in his chest. He looked again. Nothing. Had he imagined it? He stared at his mother in the rear-view mirror. She didn't look ultra-alarmed, aside from her usual apprehensive state.

Perry reclined his head and fell into another day-mare.

The next time he awoke, they were in Aurora, Illinois. The shining golden fire was already falling in the west. The road they traversed was lean and neared on both sides by long trees. Occasionally, they'd see a car pass them in the opposite direction. It was on this road that they were attacked.

A pack of nine large Mew birds descended from the clouds.

Perry's heart raced out of control.

"Hold still, Joanna," Father whispered to Mother. "They might be territorial guards. Let them scan our vehicle."

"That's an attack dive, Greg," Joanna croaked.

Perry noticed the kind of birds they were. Kites. Huge, red-tailed kites, carrying an assortment of stones and shrapnel in their talons. Before Perry could warn his father, they let the hail loose and swooped away. The stones hammered their windshield, cracking it. Lisa screamed. The shrapnel didn't seem to do any harm, and Father drove on. For a while.

Then, they skidded and stopped.

"Why are we stopping?" Joanna asked, her eyes wide with terror.

"Our tire's busted," Greg replied. He looked at Joanna. He, too, was terrified.

"They've come for him," she whispered to Father. She glanced at Perry through the rear-view mirror for a second.

"We can't be sure," replied Greg. "How did they find out? It's only been two days. This is something else. It might be the Crofts. They are good friends with the Red Tails."

The sharp cries of the birds interrupted their whispering.

Father looked up through the cracked windshield and his face turned dark.

Stones hammered their car again like a hail storm. The car jerked left and right. One large rock struck the window beside Lisa. She screamed again. Perry jumped to her, holding her still.

Joanna turned to face them. "Stay down," she said in her no-nonsense voice. "Keep her down. No matter what, do not come outside. Do not change." She flashed him a deadly look, and he knew he could never disobey that instruction.

Perry pulled Lisa to the floor behind the driver's seat. Both doors opened. Mother and Father exited the car to face the Mews who were attacking them. It didn't take long. Sounds of croaks and flaps shredded the air. Ear-splitting cries pierced their surroundings. Lisa trembled severely, sobbing. Perry wondered what she thought was happening.

He sneaked a peek from behind the seat.

It was a flurry of white, red, and blue. Rocks flew in all directions, some striking the car. He caught sight of his father's blue harrier form. It was slightly bigger than the kites. A stone hurtled towards him. He did a somersault, picking the hurtling stone out of the air and flinging it back to where it had come from. The rock struck a kite and sent it into the trees. Mother's owl form came into view. She wasn't doing too well. Two kites clipped her wings and drew her higher out of sight. Another kite blocked his view. This kite was looking into the car.

Perry tore his head away, holding his breath.

Soon, he heard something hit the car's hood. It sounded different from when it had been a stone. He looked. An owl lay, dazed, on the bonnet. About four huge kites hovered over the bird, talons poised to strike. A blue blur struck like lightning. Two kites were gone. Before the remaining two could recover, the owl sprung from the bonnet. It caught one bird by its throat and flung it away. The other bird dived headlong into the owl, sending it crashing to the asphalt ahead where the blue harrier had crashed.

It was over for Mother and Father. The huge kites hovered over their forms.

Perry's heart was pounding. He had to do something now, otherwise his parents would perish. But he couldn't disobey his mother's instruction; she had given him one of those deadly glares.

Perry glanced at Lisa. She had stopped crying, though she still shivered with dread. When those kites, whoever they were, finished with his parents, they would come for him and Lisa. He could never let anything happen to his sister, no matter what Mother had said. Never.

"Stay here, Liz," Perry whispered to her. "Don't look, okay?"

Lisa held him before he could rise. "Don't go out there, Perr," she replied, her grey eyes starting to water again.

"I have to help Mother and Father," he said. "Stay down and don't look."

Perry made his way to the front seats, wound up the windows, and left the car.

He looked. Any moment, and the kites would dive for the kill. Evening had come; in a matter of moments, it would be dark. He climbed the car until he stood on the roof. He gazed out to the nine kites, waving to get their attention. They didn't notice him. One kite struck at his mother, impaling its sharp talons into her chest. Mother gave a sharp cry. Father tried to protect Mother, but he too took a heavy impaling in his back.

Red hot anger flashed up Perry's belly.

He started with a scream and ended with an eagle whistle that tore through the air with piercing ferocity. His eyes flashed; they had never done that before. He felt the eagle rise from within him. He tried to hold it back, remembering Jake's question about changing before other Mews. But, he was far too gone. All eyes were upon him. His eagle form burst forth with a glorious white flash. It was bigger than before.

The kites scampered away from his parents, climbing the air, save one. It shot towards him with blinding speed. Perry didn't flap his wings, yet he rose into the air less than a second before being struck headlong by the kite. He clamped onto the kite's body before it shot past him. The kite struggled, wriggled, but was firmly secured at its legs and throat by Perry's claws.

The other kites squawked above him, circling in the distance. They seemed to be preparing for an assault. Perry rose to his full height of over two yards and stretched his wings all the way, revealing his true size. That did it for the kites. They fled higher and farther.

Perry looked at the red-tailed kite beneath him. It had ceased struggling. He let go, and it scampered from him and fell on the bonnet. One more look at his fully stretched form, and it lurched sideways and fell on the ground, where a trailer crushed it and zipped on; leaving grotesque red and white remains. The kites wailed in the distance before disappearing into the clouds.

Mother's owl and Father's hawk flew into the trees, probably to change. Perry jumped from the car and landed on the floor, human again.

He took one last look at the dead kite. He hadn't meant for that to happen. He had only wanted to scare them. He knew there would be war with their clan soon.

Perry ran into the car before his parents got back. He had broken his mother's word. He would pay severely.

When his parents came back, they didn't enter the car immediately. Father fixed the tire and argued with Mother at the same time. They were deciding whether to go on to New York or to take him to Africa, where their powerful relatives lived. Father insisted they keep on to New York.

They got back into the car. Father gave a sharp command for them to leave the corner where they crouched and put on their seat belts. Mother was silent, never once looking into the rear-view mirror at him. She did that when she was very mad.

Perry felt rotten. Now his mother hated him. How could one child cause so much heartache?

They stopped for the night in another motel. When he thought Perry and Lisa were asleep, Father went outside to make a call. Perry, eyes dripping tears, heard every word.

"Richard, get the twins and head to Manhattan immediately," Father said into the phone. He paused and then said, "Yes. Perry has put himself and our entire family in mortal danger. No doubt word is spreading. Before we get to the house, every Mew in the world will know of the existence of an eagle Mew. They *will* come for him." He sighed. "They will. We have to be ready."

There was another pause.

"The boy's in danger, Richard," Father finally said. "Get there, quick."

That was the last Perry heard before he was drawn into another nightmare with the sea monster.

They got to their small apartment on the Upper East Side of uptown Manhattan at dusk the following day. Richard and the twins weren't there yet. Mother hadn't talked to him the whole day, so when he finally got to his room he felt really sad. He tried calling Sarah on the phone, but she didn't pick. Sarah never ignored his calls; they were best friends.

Perry lay on his bed in the dark for a long time, hoping to hear his parents talk about him. They were silent. Sleep came later. However, it wasn't rest. It was war with the green water monster.

5

A BLAH DAY AT SCHOOL

Richard, Jake, and Jane were in their little apartment when Perry awoke the next morning. He felt weak from his bad dreams and had a slight headache. When he thought of telling his mother, he remembered that she was still mad at him. Perry wrinkled his nose, remembering how rotten he had felt yesterday and feeling the same way now.

Perry got ready for school. It wasn't so much because he loved school as it was because he wanted to see Sarah. He had already decided he would tell her. Maybe together, they could figure out this thing about the sea monster. Sarah Croft was one other person, aside from Lisa, who was effortlessly brilliant.

Perry made his way to the sitting room.

Jane was doing the dishes at the sink. Richard and Jake sat at the table with Lisa who was already halfway through her macaroni and cheese. Perry joined them. "Hi."

Jane said nothing in response but brought him a bowl of macaroni and cheese.

"I heard you saved Mother and Father," Richard whispered to Perry the moment he started on his food. His expression was blank and his tone neutral, so Perry couldn't decide whether it was a good thing or a bad thing.

"They would have been killed by all those kites," Perry whispered back, sneaking a glance at Lisa and then facing his food when he was sure she hadn't heard. He already felt so bad about it. How could he possibly feel any worse?

Richard didn't say any more.

The living room was visible from where he sat. The door that led into his parents' room was open. Mother came into the doorway, dressed in a white woolen gown and a purple jacket. She worked at a bank. She paused at the door, like she had forgotten something. Perry watched her, his heart picking pace, as her mind worked through what she had forgotten. Then her face shone with realization. But before she turned and went back the same way she came, she looked up at him.

Perry held his breath.

She flashed him a sweet smile and disappeared into the room.

Perry felt relief. He finished his food and was ready for school.

Mother and Father came into the living room. Mother smiled at him again and took his plate to the sink. She had with her a handbag. Father picked up the TV remote from the counter and turned on the TV. An image caught Perry's eye. It was that of the Hudson River. There was a greenish blur underneath the silvery surface. The caption said: *Mysterious Creature Sighted by Many*. Perry's original fears began to come back.

Jane glanced at the TV once and froze. "The sea monster," she whispered, "it has really reawakened. Who can stop it now?"

"Quiet, Jane," Mother retorted harshly, eyeing Perry and then Lisa, who was staring at the TV. Mother signaled for Father to turn it off. He did.

"There are no such things as sea monsters," Mother lied, looking at Lisa.

Richard stood and went to talk to Father. They spoke in whispers, but Perry heard them clearly.

Richard said to Father, "The seven deaths have been confirmed, and it's getting worse. Very soon, we'll be recording human casualties."

"How many more Mews thus far?" Father asked him, frowning when he caught Perry's gaze.

Perry dropped his head. He needed to learn not to look at people when he used his *super-duper* eavesdropping powers. Perry forced his head to remain bowed.

"Three more Mews so far," Richard whispered back. "Three Mews have been murdered. Their bodies were recovered from the East River. They've not been identified yet."

"That's too close to his school," Father said.

"Yeah," Richard replied. "We should take him out of the States. It might not be safe for him here anymore."

"The sea monster will follow him everywhere he goes," Father replied. "It doesn't matter if he's in the States or Africa or Australia. You know this. The only way out is to kill the monster."

"What do we do?" This was from Mother. She had joined the whispering. They had retreated further into the sitting room where Perry could not see them because of a wall. But, he heard them just as well.

"We wait," Father replied. "We wait for the chief's return." This ended the discussion. They decided that Mother and Father would take him to school, that Richard would scan the East River for the sea monster, and that Jane would drop Lisa off at school. Jake was to stand watch at home, while Perry was to come back home himself. He instantly feared the end of school.

Perry left with Mother and Father for school. He kept his eyes to the skies as they drove past all the skyscrapers. An unusual yearning for the air high above the clouds burned on the inside of him. But he knew he had to restrain himself. Even though New York was their clan's territory, and even though he had not been told *not* to transform at all, he didn't want to cause his mother any more trouble.

Their beat-up station wagon with its cracked windshield pulled up on the road beside his school's street. Perry eyed the three-story building that had CRESCENT ACADEMY splayed across the front in block letters. There were a lot of kids going into the school.

"Go on, honey," his mother said, craning her neck to look back at him. She smiled and said, "Be good. Stay out of trouble."

"Yes, Mother," Perry replied, grabbed his bag, and opened the door.

The sun was already burning its way to the top. The air was dry and warm.

"Bye, Perry," his father said before zooming off.

Perry stood alone for a while, gazing into the clouds, longing to skip school and fly away. He was about to turn when he saw the zip of a bird. He looked back and there was nothing. He thought he had seen the form of a grey hawk. He looked east, which was the direction it had gone in. Strangely, he could feel a tug to go in that direction as well. He could almost hear a call with the pull.

A stray draft of wind, fresh with the smell of the sea, caught his hair. The desire became stronger. He shoved his hands into his pocket. There was little traffic on the road, but he looked before crossing anyway. Mother had commanded him never to cross a road without looking, even if it was abandoned. He marched down the sidewalk beside the school's fence along with the other students. Ahead, he saw freckled blonde hair, a light pink jacket, and the pale grey jeans that Sarah only wore when she was excited.

"Sarah!" he shouted, pushing through the bodies in his front. "Sarah!"

Sarah turned, a frown on her face.

Perry skidded to a halt one yard away from her. Two of her friends stood beside her, frowning at him as well.

Perry didn't understand. What was she mad at him for?

"What is it, Perry Johnson?" She spat out his name as though it were a venomous substance. Her blue eyes were as startling as ever.

Perry stammered, utterly stonewalled. He didn't usually need a reason to call her; things just sort of came up as they discussed them.

Sarah cocked her eyebrow. "Well?" she sneered, making him look like a fool. "Are you just going to stand there?"

Perry felt a rush of blood up his cheek. The stream of students around them descended into a blur of colorful shirts.

"I...I wanted to..." Perry couldn't remember why he had called her. Why would he, an average nobody, call someone as intelligent, rich, and stunning as Sarah Croft? They had nothing in common. To think they were besties before the last weekend made him feel all the more foolish.

She flashed him an icy, wicked look. "Stay away from me, Perry Johnson," she scowled, wheeled around, and fell into the blur. Her friends did the same.

Perry stood, rooted to the ground, unable to move, unable to think. He felt so stupid.

He heard a bell ring. It was faint. Somewhere in his mind, he knew he should be in class by now.

"Hey, kid, you coming or what?" said Mr. Bart, their school's security man.

Perry looked around. The man stood at the gate, holding it ajar. The sidewalk was deserted. Perry ran into the school.

The whole day was a blur. Mrs. Blueberry, his Latin teacher, humiliated him for his ineptitude at a language no one had spoken for thousands of years. Mr. Foley, his mathematics tormentor, was kind (or horrible,

Perry couldn't tell), asking the whole class questions and never him. It was as if his teachers got a message the night before saying: *Perry Johnson is a dullard; HUMILIATE WHEN POSSIBLE.*

Not once did Sarah look back at him during class.

During lunch, Perry tried to talk to her again. She screamed and got him an after-school detention. He wasn't supposed to get detention. At least not for trying to talk to a friend. But, Sarah's parents were rich. And so naturally, the principal felt Perry was stalking a student. "Inappropriate behavior," Mr. Noel had rebuked.

At the end of school, Perry could feel himself drowning in his own sorrow. He stood at the gate, waiting for Sarah to come out. He wasn't going to talk to her. He just wanted to see her; he wanted her to see him. Students whirred past him; his eyes scanned the multitude for a pink jacket. He caught one at the steps.

Sarah descended the steps with her two friends in tow. Perry's first urge was to go talk to her. But then he remembered Mr. Noel's threat of expulsion. He had brought his family shame. He would do so no more.

A black Ferrari pulled up by the school gate just as Sarah got there. She passed by Perry without as much as a glance in his direction. When Sarah got to the vehicle, the driver came out and hugged her. It was Don, Sarah's older brother. Sarah and her two friends entered the car. Before Don entered the vehicle, he turned and glanced at him. His eyes were full of hatred. So full that Perry flinched. Don got in the car then drove off.

"Mr. Johnson," the principal called from the top of the stairs. The crowd had thinned.

Perry turned to face him. "Yes, Mr. Noel."

"Your detention starts now, Mr. Johnson."

"Yes, Mr. Noel." Perry walked up to meet him.

It was six when he was finally let go. The outside was barely bright when he got to the gate. Perry hesitated at the see-through iron, searching the skies. Four Mew-sized birds roamed the clouds above him. He couldn't tell who they were. Fear gripped him like an electric shock.

"Hey, kid!"

Perry jerked away from the sound, turning to look. He saw it was just the security man.

"You got to go, kid," the plump man said, sitting in a chair behind the security post. "No kids allowed on school grounds past six."

Perry looked up again. Four birds looked down at him. He could see their eyes. They weren't friends. They were foes. Yesterday, Father had said word would spread and that people would come for him. This was proof. He was no longer safe anywhere. Perry looked at the security man again. Mr. Bart's eyes were now glowering with anger. How could Perry tell him that his life was in danger at the hands of four birds? Perry would just sound crazy and that could get him more detention.

Perry stepped outside the gate and made a run for the bus station. The birds dived and followed. Instantly, Perry was overwhelmed with a desire to transform and show those birds who was boss, but his mother's words held him in check. When the bus pulled out of the station, it was fully dark.

Perry thought he had lost the birds because when he got off at his stop, they were no longer in flight. But he knew they could be hiding behind those dark clouds above. Unfortunately, the night lights of Manhattan did not reach far into the sky.

Perry ran the rest of the way to his parents' apartment.

6

RUN PERRY!
IT'S A TRAP!

Perry barged into his home, exhausted and out of breath.

"Where have you been?" Richard shot up from the dinner table. Jane and Jake remained seated looking at him, worried.

"I called your school," Richard said, stepping closer. His grey eyes burned with fury. Perry held from turning and running. "They said you left school at six." Richard looked at the clock on the wall. "It is almost seven thirty. Where have you been?"

Perry's chest heaved. His lungs were aflame, and the dry air didn't help. "I walked," Perry replied. He didn't want to tell them about the birds. He didn't want to look like a fool, like how Sarah had made him look. He was still hurting.

"You walked?!" Richard exploded.

Perry flinched. He had never seen Richard this mad at him before. Somehow, Perry felt that something had changed. Something about the sea monster.

"With all that's going on with the—" Richard paused, looking away. The green papered walls met his gaze. "Go into your room and get changed," Richard said without looking at him.

Perry kept his head down and trudged to his room. He hadn't told Richard the reason why he had walked. When he returned to the dining room, Jake was no longer there.

Richard and Jane were whispering, but then they saw him enter and stopped.

Perry's suspicions grew.

Jane rose to her feet. She flashed him a smile and went to the kitchen. "Your food is cold. You're just going to have to manage it."

Perry sat down with Richard. Lisa was in the sitting room doing her assignments. The fact that he felt unhappy and still had loads of assignments to do annoyed him.

"Where's Mother and Father?" Perry asked. They were supposed to be back by now.

"Clan chief called them. Clan meeting," Richard replied. Perry wasn't fooled. He could feel Richard's dread wax strong.

The only reason they would be holding a clan meeting was to decide his fate. He still didn't know why he was in danger. But the fact that Richard was scared terrified him.

"Is it about the sea monster?"

Plates rattled in the kitchen. Perry briefed a glance at Jane; she had frozen.

Richard placed his hand on the table, creating folds on his T-shirt. "Clan chief called a meeting." His voice was firm, though it held no anger. There would be no more discussion on the subject. However, Perry's suspicions were confirmed. Something terrible had happened. Something about the sea monster.

The atmosphere in the house grew gloomier.

Jane set Perry's food before him.

Perry frowned at the stale, milky soup. They weren't the rich sort, he got it. But, did it have to get this bad? Or was this punishment for coming home late?

Perry picked up his spoon and started eating.

Richard's phone rang. "Hello?"

Richard dropped the call and stood.

"Father called," he said to Jane. "I have to join him."

Jane nodded.

Richard turned and headed for the door.

Perry finished his soup with turmoil in his heart. He tried to rid himself of the way he felt. He felt afraid. Uncertain. Caged. He hated these emotions. They were for weak people. He wasn't smart, but he wasn't weak either.

Back in his room, Perry sat crossed-legged on the rug before his bed. He pulled his bag from the bed where he had thrown it to the ground and removed his books. He found a pen in one of the many holds and began on his homework. Distraction didn't help. He caught himself drifting away in thoughts more times than he cared to count. He had assignments in social studies, math, and science due this week. Yet, he hadn't gotten far in any of them.

Perry kicked his books away. He stood and paced his small room. Through the window in the wall, bright lights came into his room. Lights from tall buildings, street lampposts, streaming vehicles, the drum of traffic, the yells of mad drivers, the honking of cars; these sounds filtered into his room with a strange, soothing rhythm. Perry pulled closer to the window. He looked through the catwalk to the distant skyscrapers. His gaze strayed up, towards the dark clouds. The bright moon passed in and out like a divine weave.

His heart tugged at him. He wanted to fly. He yearned to fly.

Perry turned away, sighing aloud to relieve the tension in his body. He felt weak. He needed to rest. He made it to the bed.

A tap on his shoulder woke him later.

He moaned lightly, still groggy. Jane crouched beside him, her black lustrous hair clouding her face. "It's time for dinner," she said, "come on."

Perry got up and followed her to the dining room. He looked at the clock. He had slept for three hours. It sure felt like three minutes.

Richard, Mother, and Father were not back yet.

He wanted to ask why, but when he saw Lisa eating at the table, he refrained from talking. Maybe if she wasn't there, Jane or Jake would be more inclined to tell him why.

Perry found his place at the table and joined the solemn assembly to eat. Dinner was hot as promised, but it was the same milky soup.

As he ate, he studied the twins. They traded worried glances from time to time.

Lisa ate, oblivious to their concerns. When she was through, she excused herself and went to bed.

"Why aren't they back?" Perry asked, looking directly at Jake. He had short, saltpeter hair and a boxy face, and he didn't look at Perry or answer him.

Perry's annoyance grew. Jake was merely four years older than Perry. He had no right to keep him in the dark concerning their parents' safety. Perhaps, being an eagle meant he was the most powerful Mew amongst the trio. If Father or Mother or Richard needed saving, he should be the natural choice to save them.

"Why aren't they back, Jake?" he asked again, an edge in his voice.

Jake flashed him a warning glare. "Eat your food, Perry."

Perry dropped his spoon with a splatter. "Answer me first," he said, raising his voice.

Jake smashed his knuckles into the table, sending his plate and its content into the air for a second. "Eat your food, Perry!" he yelled.

Jane recoiled in the chair, startled.

Perry pushed the plate away from himself, pushed away from the table, and stormed out of the living room. Back in his room, in the dark, he fought back tears but failed. He sat facing the window, sobbing.

When the tears stopped coming, the skies called out to him. This time, he responded.

First, he shut the door to his room. Then, he raised the window and crawled onto the catwalk. The thing creaked and shook under him. Perry held himself, motionless, waiting for the thing to steady. He then stood erect, high above the ground and closed his eyes, spreading out his hands. The cold winds buffeted his body right, left, and center. The sharp honks, yells, and traffic faded into the background as he concentrated on the rise of the eagle within him.

When he opened his eyes, they flashed. All that remained was for him to jump.

The fall was ten stories high. A normal person would be scared at this height. But, Perry was no normal person. He was a Mew. An eagle Mew.

Perry drew a deep breath, his heart suddenly pounding. *What if it didn't work this time?* He threw himself into the air and fell.

It didn't take long. He transformed and swooped up through the air, rising.

The air formed around him, and he gathered speed. His first instinct was the clouds. With each flap of his massive wings, the earth retreated away from him with great speed. The noise of traffic ceased. The roads became lines that seemed to flow because of the traffic. He flapped higher. The clouds met him, and they too began to descend below him. The temperature fell deadly low. Icicles began to develop along the length of his wings.

Yet, he flapped higher.

Through the clouds, the skyscrapers were tiny dots of lights. The Hudson River, the East River, these had all disappeared. The air became thin. Perry struggled to breathe, nonetheless, moving his wings with immense strain, higher. Until there was nothing left to breathe and the moon stood just above his head: a giant, dirty, bright ball. He was in space.

Perry ceased flapping, satisfied, and fell.

It took him less time to get to the Earth than it took him to get to space. He pierced the air, his wings housed near his body, with the speed of a bullet. High above the Chrysler Building, he whistled as loud as his lungs would allow. He swooped as low as four yards above the ground and flew above cars, whistling. Heads turned. Hands pointed. Everyone marveled at him. They had never seen an eagle so large.

Near the Empire State Building, he swooped into the air, formed his wings around his body, and spun higher into the air. Cheers came from the crowd that had gathered. He then spread his wings and climbed the air along the side of the building. At the top, he perched on the lightning conductor, resting his wings on the smooth slope at the base of the cold metal. To the crowd below, he would just be an anomalous shape disfiguring the sharp spike of the lightning conductor, but Perry could see them clearly. Their faces shone with amusement as they peered up at him. Perry's heart was awash with excitement.

Perry knew they wouldn't see it clearly, but he did it anyway. He lifted his wings away from the building and spread it full length. The only things that attached him to the building were his talons. They held tightly, even against the fast winds that battered his feathers. Flashes of cameras came to him from below. Perry basked in the exhilaration for a moment.

A thought crossed his mind. He looked south, and a darkness descended upon him.

He pushed from the building into the embrace of the winds and glided in that direction. He kept south until he came to a street in West Village. Beautiful houses with neatly trimmed lawns lined cleanly paved streets. The streets were mostly deserted. The neighborhood was nice and quiet.

Perry circled a house for a while, uncertain of himself. It stood, white and blue, along a line of white and blue houses. It had two floors and a garage. There seemed to be no sounds coming from the house.

There's no need, he thought. Even if she wasn't asleep, she had made it pretty clear that she didn't want to have anything to do with him. Why was he there, then?

Perry circled once more, scanning his environment for signs of trouble. When he saw that there were no Mew birds around, he perched on the roof of the house across the street from Sarah's. He saw her through the window. Her room could have easily contained their whole apartment. It was a large room above the second level. She lay on her belly on the bed reading. Her hair was drawn back in a ponytail. Her legs were up in the air swinging back and forth.

The room was well lit with a pink décor. Perry fidgeted on the blue roof. His sharp claws gave a *tak-tak-tak* sound that unnerved him.

Perry finally decided and whistled at Sarah.

She stiffened visibly in her bed but remained focused on the paper before her. She quickly picked up a pen and started scribbling. When she was done, she raised it up in his direction. In bold block letters, Sarah had written: RUN PERRY! IT'S A TRAP!

Perry's blood curdled.

He jerked a step back and turned just in time to see a Mew-sized falcon descend upon him, claws poised, but not in time to prevent it. Perry watched helplessly as the dagger-sharp claws closed on his throat. Higher beyond, another falcon hovered, no doubt waiting to share in his meat. Perry knew it was over for him.

In a split second, another bird—a grey hawk—smashed into the falcon, both birds spiraling off the roof.

"*Run, Perry!*" Richard boomed over their clan communication link. "*Run!*"

Perry sprung from the roof and climbed the air, shooting upwards at a frightening speed. His brother disengaged from the stunned falcon and followed, flying low. The two falcons fell in behind them and pursued.

7

THE OLD MAN
WITH THE
STRANGE VOICE

They raced across Manhattan. Perry gained distance each second.

Perry flew high and fast, his sharp beak piercing the air at over one-hundred miles per hour. Richard flew low and slow, guarding the rear. Way behind him, the two falcons trailed. Perry could see their eyes from this distance; they were dark and menacing. *What did I ever do to them?* he wondered.

When he passed the Empire State Building, neither Richard nor the falcons were in view behind. He circled high above the lightning conductor, searching dark clouds for miles in the direction he had come; he didn't see a gray hawk or the evil falcons. His first thought was to go back. But then he decided against it and continued northeast.

In minutes, their apartment building came into view. The window was still wide open—just enough space to scrape through if he bellied in his wings.

Perry swooped a little into the air, breaking his forward motion. He spun, his wings forming a cape around his body, until his head was positioned in the direction of the room. Then, he shot right for the window. The moment he was through the catwalk, he transformed back into human form, grazing the rug with a yelp. He lay on the floor for a while, chest heaving below him.

His parents broke into his room.

"Perry!" His mother rushed to meet him.

Perry cringed back, bracing for a slap on his face. But she pulled him from the floor and hugged him tightly. "Are you all right?" she asked, looking into his eyes. "What happened?" Genuine concern was evident in her eyes.

Tears formed in Perry's eyes, and he began to sob. He had almost died tonight was what happened. One more second, and the falcons would have killed him. One more second. Mother hugged him again. This time, Perry held her too. Father placed a hand on his head.

Another bird came through the window, transforming into a human on his knees.

Richard shot to his feet and swiveled to face Perry. His face was contorted with fury. "DO YOU WANT TO GET YOURSELF KILLED?!"

Perry stiffened, burying his head in his mother's body. The room shook with his brother's scorn.

"It's okay, Richard," his mother said in a low, soothing tone.

"No, it's not okay, Mother!" Richard replied, still angry. "Perry almost got himself killed!"

Tension rose in the room.

"Outside, now," Father said, walking out of the room.

Richard left with Father, but his mother remained, holding him. After a while, Perry broke from his mother, left her on the rug, and slithered into his bed. He pulled the sheets over his body, shivering in the cold wind from the open window. He felt weak, tired, and confused. And angry.

His mother stood from where she lay on the floor and closed the window, latching it properly.

"Perr," she said at his side, "it's over. You're safe here. I'll never let anything bad happen to you. I promise. Your brother, Richard, will come around tomorrow, all right?"

Perry nodded, shutting his eyes.

"I love you, honey," she said and kissed him on his forehead.

"I love you too, Mother," he muttered as she rose from the bed and walked to the door.

Perry almost fell asleep and missed the grim news. Almost. In fact, he wished he had.

It only took five minutes after Mother had left. The voices came to his ears, clear, but in whispers.

Mother was angry. "What happened, Richard? You were supposed to be protecting him!"

"I was," Richard retorted. His breathing was elevated. "I was circling the building when a red-tailed kite appeared from nowhere. I had to chase it away. Perry must have left the house at that time because I caught sight of him when I pulled from my chase and followed him."

"How could you go so far away from the house?" Mother replied, obviously enraged by his excuse. "You were supposed to be on the defensive not offensive. What if it was a trap?"

Richard had no reply to this.

"What if it was a trap? Answer me!"

"Joanna," his father cautioned.

"Don't, Greg!" Mother said. "Richard?"

"I'm sorry, Mother," Richard said, mellowed, a twinge of fear in his voice. "It won't happen again."

"There won't be a next time for you, Richard," Mother said, a little calm. "I'm never trusting you with my son's life again."

"Mother!"

"No more, Richard. That's the end of it."

There was an edgy silence.

"What happened?" Father asked.

Richard sighed. "He went to the Crofts—"

"What?!" Mother breathed.

"—he doesn't know about us and the Crofts, Mother. Sarah Croft is his classmate and close friend from what I can tell. Sarah's brothers almost slew him on the roof today, and it wasn't just so they could get his powers. It was different. They wanted revenge."

Perry unhooked from the silent conversation for a while. He was excited and dismayed both at the same time. Excited that Sarah could and most probably was a Mew. Dismayed that her brothers, Don and Chase, both falcons, would try to kill him. He had known Don and Chase all his life. Why would they suddenly turn evil?

"This cannot go unpunished, Father," Jake said.

"I agree with Jake, Father," Jane said. "We can't let the Crofts push us too far. We need to strike back."

"There's no need for a war now, especially with the sea monster loose and getting stronger," Mother replied softly. "The most important thing is that Perry is alive."

"That's not the most important thing, Joanna," Father replied, his tone tight. "This attack is an effrontery to our authority. It was conducted on New York soil—in our territory, Joanna. If we don't reply in kind, it would mean we are weak, afraid. We can't let it go. The Crofts have to leave this city or pay for their impudence with blood."

Another tense silence.

Perry's heart was already doing thirty miles per hour.

"Aren't we forgetting the main issue here?" said a strange voice. "The boy has to know."

The voice was strange in two ways. One, Perry had never heard it before. Two, it sounded funny: weak, like it belonged to an old man, yet strong, like it contained power.

"About eagles, or about the sea monster?" Father asked, punctuating the sentence with sighs.

"Both," said the strange voice.

Silence.

"Everything?" Father asked.

"No," Mother pleaded. "We can't tell him everything. It'll kill him. There must be another way."

"There's no other way, Jo." The strange voice called his mother's name with a fondness that could only mean family. "This afternoon the monster attacked a civilian cruiser off the coast of Long Island—"

"The headline said it was minor turbulence," Jane pointed out.

"Minor turbulences don't kill Mews!" The old man bellowed. What followed was a short, acidic silence.

The old man resumed with a voice so full of pain that Perry began to sob silently. "The chief had the Nelsons and the Bryans on aerial patrol duty when they sighted the hydro cyclone approaching the coast. Most ships were berthed and deserted, but one was still deep on the sea. The patrol team sent Bobby Bryan—the Bryans' initiate—to call for help while they held the monster at bay. Help didn't come in time, and Bobby's parents perished at the hands of the creature. This is why the clan meeting ended in an impasse. On the day that the monster rose, seven Mews patrolling the Georgian coast were killed. The day following, three more died. Now this. That's twelve Mews dead already, Jo. We are being slaughtered, and it needs to stop!" The old man's bitter voice ceased for a moment.

In the rancorous silence that ensued, Perry's heart burned with hurt. He knew Bobby's parents—he and Bobby had attended Middle School together—they were nice people and didn't deserve to die. He had re-awakened the monster; their deaths were on his head.

"There will be a general clan meeting tomorrow by the will of the Council," the old man continued, his voice soft. "The Mews' next course of action will be decided. Perry is the eagle. It has to be him."

A window opened. Perry heard boisterous winds accompanied by flapping clothes.

"Jo, Greg, the sooner, the better."

There was a transformation. A bird soared away, and the window was closed.

Father was the first person to break the uneasy silence that followed. "The clan chief wants us and Richard to represent the clan at the meeting. There is the possibility of a bloodbath. Lisa is not safe in New York."

"I'll take her to our cliff house in Nevada," Jane cut in. "We'll remain there until things cool down."

"What about Perry?" Mother asked, a fear in her voice. "There will be strange Mews flying the skies now that the meeting is in New York. Perry will be hunted like game. Leaving him here would be suicidal."

"Perry has to remain in town, Joanna," Father replied. "The chief has commanded it. Until a decision is reached, Perry has come under the protection of the Council."

"Come on, Greg," Mother sneered. "You know that that's about as effective as fighting fire with gasoline. It didn't stop the Crofts today. It won't stop other Mews tomorrow."

"What if they rule against his favor?" Richard asked.

"Then so be it," Father said, his voice devoid of emotion.

Mother gasped, "But he's just a boy!"

"If he has to do it," Father said, "then he can do it. I trust *my* boy."

Perry felt a rush of courage at his father's words. Never had he been trusted for anything. But now, his father trusted him. His father trusted him to solve this sea monster issue. He was the eagle. It was his responsibility. He would not fail. No, he would not.

Perry sat up in his bed, itching to make full proof of his father's trust in him. Any Mew who stood in front of him would be crushed by his wings. Perry was angry now. There would be no more running. He would stand and fight. Let the evil birds come.

"But can he?" Richard's voice came to his ears.

Mother sobbed, light. "What if he can't? What if he fails? I can't lose another son, Greg."

Father must have embraced Mother, because he spoke words of comfort to her next, and his words were like a healing salve on a hurting wound. "We aren't going to lose Perry, Jo. Tomorrow's meeting will determine our next course of action." This ended their discussion for the night.

Perry lay back down on the bed. *Another son?*

In his dreams that night, Perry was flying again. Soaring above the night. At first, he enjoyed the rush of air through his feathers and wings. He enjoyed the aerial view of Manhattan with its night lights. Then, he realized he wasn't flying of his own accord. He was being pulled. He panicked and tried to change course, but he couldn't. When he looked down again, he saw that he was flying over the Atlantic Ocean into the deep. The face of the water was covered in a dark mist. A foreboding feeling cloaked him like a shield. In the black haze, he saw flickers of a creature moving among the surface waves. It was green and serpentine.

Perry tried to scream and whistle for help, but his beak remained closed.

He never saw the creature fully. What he saw next was a ghastly parted maw and the sharp and crooked outline of teeth, all covered in a fetid dark haze. A great, irresistible suction pulled Perry into the creature's mouth. To his death.

Silence and nothingness followed.

Then said a malevolent voice out of the void: *this is what awaits you, Eagle. You can't resist me. I won't come to you, but you will come to me.*

Perry awoke, gasping.

8

PERRY IS ATTACKED

Mother, Father, Lisa, and Jane were already gone when Perry showed up at the dining room table for breakfast. Sunlight streamed into the room from the window opposite the living room. The door was ajar, and neither Richard nor Jake seemed to think this was a bad thing. Dry air filled the room.

Perry settled in the chair, placing his backpack on the other chair. He wore a black jacket over a gray T-shirt and brown pants. The material that Mother had given to him in their motel room in Aurora was tucked neatly in his back pocket. He had never let go of it since that time.

Jake dropped a plate on the table. There were three slices of pizza on it. Perry looked up at Jake with a frown.

Jake shrugged, his rough saltpeter hair wriggling. "Mother and Father aren't around. Be happy you get to eat." He placed on the table a glass of water and walked away.

Richard came into the house. He had on the same gray T-shirt he wore the day before. In his hands was a large set of keys. "Lisa and Jane are already out of the city. I followed them as far as Union City," he said aloud to Jake.

"Have things heated up yet?" Jake stood by the sink.

Richard nodded. "More than we anticipated. Met about six Mews I've never seen before. They may have attacked if the Fortins weren't with me." Richard settled down at the dining table, still looking at Jake.

"The Fortins are in town?" Jake asked with a smile on his face.

"Yes, they are," Richard replied. "They came with their son. I heard he's Perry's age. Turned into a huge falcon."

Jake grinned now. "Sweet!"

Richard turned to face Perry. His smile vanished. "Perry, I'm sorry I got mad at you yesterday. It wasn't your fault. It was mine."

Perry remained silent and kept on eating. He didn't look up at Richard.

"I know you have a lot of questions about what happened yesterday," Richard continued. "I'm going to try and answer your questions before you go to school.

"The sea monster is a creature of immense evil and darkness. It has plagued Mewranters for centuries before us. It has never been defeated, only subdued. That's why everyone is so afraid of the creature. There will be a general clan meeting tonight where we will decide what to do about the sea monster. Hopefully, before tomorrow, the threat should be destroyed. Now, general clan meetings are dangerous meetings, so Jane has taken Lisa to the safety of our cliff house in Nevada. You, however, have to stay since the meeting is more or less about you.

"Are you done eating?"

"Yes," Perry replied, getting to his feet and strapping his bag to his back.

Richard led him out the door and down the stairs to where their beat-up station wagon was parked in the road, still warm from use. Perry looked up instinctively. The sky was clear and devoid of life; no birds, Mew or normal. The sun was blazing in the east, its bright streaks split by several skyscrapers.

"Perry!"

Perry's gaze dropped to the world of men, to Richard's blank face. Richard was standing by the car while he was still on the sidewalk. People passed by in both directions, giving him only a fleeting moment of their attention.

"Get in," Richard said, motioning with his head.

Perry left the sidewalk, walked around the car, and got into the vehicle. There was still a crack in the windshield.

They drove to school. Perry constantly searched the skies, oblivious to his brother's presence or wandering stares at him. He caught sight of several Mew-sized birds along the way, flying very high and beyond Richard's eyesight. They didn't seem to be following them.

Perry saw a huge black falcon zip in and out of his line of sight. Instead of following the Mew bird, he cringed back into his seat, remembering his encounter from yesterday. He couldn't remember the color of the birds that had attacked him yesterday; all he knew was that they were falcons.

As they neared the school, Richard began to talk again. All he had said so far Perry already knew. But there were still a lot of things he didn't know about himself and the sea monster. He had already decided he would only learn these things by hearing them being discussed in the night.

"Perry, listen to me," Richard said, eyes on the traffic. "It isn't safe in New York for any hatchling now. There are a lot of different clans present in Manhattan alone. You have to desist from transforming. Keep out of the skies. Stay away from bodies of water. And stay near people. When school closes, take the bus to the house. Don't go elsewhere, and you won't get attacked."

Richard parked the car opposite of the school. At the same moment, a black Lexus sedan pulled up by the school gate. The driver, a man in a black suit, got out of the car and opened the passenger's door. Sarah stepped out, thanking the chauffeur. She waved him goodbye as he drove off.

Richard said in a low, ominous tone, pulling in close to Perry, "A war is brewing between the clans. You must choose your friends wisely. Stay out of trouble, especially Mew trouble. When trouble comes knocking, run away. You might be an eagle, but you cannot best two powerful falcons."

Richard pulled away and looked at the road. "Go."

Perry opened the car and stepped into the sun. He crossed the road, joining the stream of other students. When the bell rang, he was seated in class, behind Sarah Croft.

Richard's instructions resounded in his mind throughout school. Richard hadn't said it, but Sarah Croft was the enemy. At least her brothers were. They had tried to kill him yesterday. Now, Perry wasn't sure he should be near Sarah even though that was what he wanted. Her streaked blonde hair lit up brilliantly in the sunlight. She wore a brown blouse and white jeans. Perry stayed away from her until school ended when he couldn't take it anymore.

"Sarah!" Perry ran up the sidewalk beside school. Sarah ignored him; she walked ahead, waiting for her chauffeur to come pick her up.

"Sarah!" Perry caught up with her and stood in front of her, blocking her path.

Other kids pushed past them. Perry ignored this. He was pulled in by Sarah's startling blue eyes. They swirled with emotions.

"What is it, Perry Johnson?" Sarah said, without the venom. "You want to get another detention?" In her voice, there was no jeer, no taunt: only frustration, pain.

Perry felt a tug for the skies. He focused on Sarah's face, ignoring the urge to transform into the eagle. "Your brothers tried to kill me yesterday, Sarah, and you saved me. What's this all about? I thought we were enemies now. Or did they tell you to stay away from me?"

Sarah heaved a sigh of frustration and looked away. She did that when Perry was right. "You don't know the half of it, Perr. Stay away from me. Your life depends on it." She started walking again.

Perry watched her walk into the thin forest beside their school, her pink bag jerking slightly behind her. He was shocked by her response. She didn't deny that her brothers had tried to kill him yesterday. Perry was afraid, immediately realizing that the threat to his life was real. He had a decision to make. But he had already made it yesterday. No more running. It was time to stand and fight. Father trusted him; he would not fail.

Perry ran into the forest after Sarah.

"Sarah," Perry said when he caught up with her. They walked side by side. "Sarah, I'm tired of running. I'm tired of cowering and hiding. This has to stop. I'm going to fight. You can either fight with me or fight against me, but you can't ignore me. You've got to talk to me, Sarah."

Sarah stopped and stared at him for a while. "You might be an eagle, Perr, but you are still a hatchling. When my brother finds out that we are still friends, they'll tear you to pieces."

Perry's heart leaped to his throat. "I'll take my chances with the falcons. So I take it we aren't enemies anymore?"

Sarah nodded with a smile. They continued walking. Tall trees loomed over them, widely dispersed. Brown, withered leaves carpeted the ground. The sunset set the area ablaze with strokes of golden light.

"The little scene in school yesterday," Sarah said, hesitating, searching the ground for words. "I was compelled to do it. When I heard that you were an eagle Mew, I thought the only way to protect you from my family was to stay away from you. It pained me, Perr. I'm sorry."

"It's okay," Perry replied, glancing at her. A teardrop had etched a line down her left cheek. He changed the topic. "Why is it such a bad thing to be an eagle? Why did your brothers attack me?"

They got to a cliff that overlooked a beach. They settled on the edge, their legs dangling in the air. Their bags were dumped in a heap beside them.

Sarah drew in a deep breath. "Perry, there has not been an eagle for over a thousand years. Little is known about eagle Mews. No one knows what an eagle's true potential is. There are rumors about eagles. Rumors that say eagle Mews are the end of the Mew lineage. Of course, all that is bogus. Still, people are scared."

Perry managed to find the words. "A thousand years," he echoed, his eyes lost in the endless waves of the sea.

"It's not that there haven't been hatchlings. There have been five or six in the last century. It's just that no eagle Mew makes it past the age of sixteen. They either meet with a terrible fate, or they are killed. I'm sorry, Perr, but life expectancy for eagle Mews is really short." Her face darkened with sadness.

Perry felt sadder. It was his life on the line. "So, people just kill eagle Mews whenever they are born, because they don't understand enough about them?"

Sarah gave a smile of sarcasm. "That's pretty much it—oh, and when you kill an eagle Mew, you absorb a measure of their power. Makes you stronger than most."

Perry cocked his eyebrow in realization. That was the reason why he was being hunted. He was a Mew energy booster. The whole news weighed heavily on his heart.

"There seems to be friction between your family and mine. And I think it's beyond me being an eagle. Richard said your brothers didn't attack me because they wanted my powers. He said that they attacked me because they wanted revenge. I don't understand. Revenge for what? I didn't do anything to them."

Sarah nodded once and looked away. "It's not you, Perr. It's a blood feud that has existed between our families for years. My mom doesn't talk about it much. But, that's all my brothers talk about. Someone died in my family and now my brothers want the same in yours. That's why they are after you. Be careful, Perr. They will stop at nothing to kill you."

A gloom began to descend on them, so Perry changed the subject. "What did you turn into?"

"What?" Sarah faced him, her eyes blinking in confusion.

"The ritual? What is your aerial form?"

Sarah's brows arched. "Oh. I'm a white owl, just like your mother. Want to see?"

Perry nodded. They stood up.

Sarah stood on the ledge, pushed off its edge, and fell through the air. She fell like a log of tree, her hands spread like a bird. Then, her form began to change. Beak replaced mouth, feathers replaced skin, wings replaced hands, and Sarah soared into the air: a giant white owl.

Excited, Perry jumped off the cliff to join her. His eagle form came faster, like a lion that had been caged in starvation. He shot after Sarah, and together they flew in and out of the forest. They flew high and low. They flew fast and slow. They flew along the beach and along the tree line.

As Perry bathed in the tumultuous rush of air that attended his speed, he felt a release of tension in his heart. He was no longer afraid of fighting as long as Sarah fought alongside him. Sarah flew beside him, matching him speed for speed, move for move. They flew in perfect sync, as though they were a single unit.

They were flying back towards the cliff when Perry saw a black falcon high up in the setting sun—descending towards them, claws poised to snatch flesh. Sarah was flying less than a yard below him; they were about fifty yards above the ground. Perry pretended he hadn't seen the bird and flew on.

When the falcon was upon them, Sarah sensed it and dropped, letting the wind push her backwards in a veering motion. But Perry spun with blinding speed to face the falcon, startling the creature for a second. Their claws met with a *zing!*

They hung in the air, slapping each other with their wings and striking their claws together. The falcon was big and strong, but Perry was bigger and stronger. He overpowered the falcon, mounting it as they fell to the ground. Before he hit the sand, he transformed back and held the falcon's throat with his bare hands. The falcon choked, squirming its enormous feathers, creating wind.

Somewhere behind him, he heard Sarah's voice. "Perry, no!" she said, running towards him.

Perry ignored her. He raised a fist to strike the falcon's head when it began to transform. Perry pinned it to the ground the whole way and found himself on top of a black boy who couldn't have been older than himself.

The boy raised his hands to protect his face from Perry's impending strike. "Please, don't kill me," the boy said, his voice tiny and breathless, fear in his eyes.

9

JAMES FORTIN:
THE INFORMANT

Perry held his fist in the air, not yet willing to let the boy go. "Why did you attack us?!" Perry roared, causing the boy to cringe deeper into the sand.

Sarah came to a halt by his side. "Perry, let him go," she said, short of breath. Her face was moist, and so strands of her tousled hair stuck to her forehead.

Perry ignored her. He observed the boy with a cross-examining eye. He was as tall as Perry with a round face and slightly bulging, anticipatory eyes. There was something about this boy, Perry realized. He had a smirk on his face, like he enjoyed being under a raised fist.

Perry frowned. Realizing that the boy had no intention of answering his question, he let him go and sat down opposite him. Sarah settled on the ground beside Perry, and together they watched as the falcon picked himself from the sand and sat before them.

"I'm sorry I attacked you," the boy said, his voice carrying a drawl. He was smiling excitedly. "I heard there was an eagle Mew in Manhattan. I wanted to see for myself."

"Who are you?" Sarah asked, calm, her hair wriggling in the soft wind from the sea.

"James Fortin," the boy replied.

Surprise came on Sarah's face. "*The* Fortin?" she said, her voice tainted with incredulity.

James nodded. "My parents are in town for the meeting tonight. They brought me along."

Sarah turned to Perry. "The Fortins are legendary elite Mews—"

"Hold on," Perry interrupted her. "What's an elite Mew?"

James looked at Perry in disbelief. "You don't know what an elite Mew is? Where have you been? Under a rock?" He smirked.

Naturally, Perry shouldn't have been angered by this statement, but the smirk did it for him. Before he could say or do anything to retaliate, Sarah spoke.

"Elite Mews are like soldiers," Sarah said without so much as a glance James's way. "If Mews were civilians, elite Mews would be soldiers. If Mews were soldiers, elite Mews would be black ops. Something like that. The Fortins aren't just ordinary elite Mews. They're legendary."

"How do you know all these things and I don't?" Perry was beginning to feel average again.

Sarah shrugged. "I took lessons after my fall. It's standard practice for every Mew. In your case, I can understand why your parents would skip the lessons for now, you being an eagle and all."

Perry took the reply half-heartedly, still thinking it was more than that. He started to say something to James when James spoke up.

"Your parents didn't tell you anything about eagle Mews, did they?"

Perry instantly became guarded. He didn't want James to think he was ignorant about his abilities. Still, he wanted to know what James knew. There was something about the way James spoke that told Perry he knew about eagle Mews.

"They didn't tell you about the sea monster either?" James's eyes searched and probed Perry's. He added, squinting his eyes, "About the connection between you and the sea monster?" His voice dropped to a whisper. "About the pull you feel towards the sea?"

Perry looked at Sarah. She gave him a shrug. She didn't know about any of this.

"About the dreams?"

Perry threw his hands into the air in frustration. "All right, all right," he breathed. "You win. I don't know jack about any of this. I need to know. Please tell me."

James Fortin smiled. He then nodded and became serious. He looked at the falling sun before he began. His eyes squinted; he seemed to be re-calling some extraneous detail about Perry's predicament. He looked at Perry once more.

"I'm not from New York," he said, looking between Sarah and Perry. "I'm from Massachusetts. I've lived in Boston with my parents since I was born. We have our Fall Ritual in Boston. For years, kids our age have been initiated into Mew clans all around the world. But never has it been understood why it is that when an eagle Mew is born the sea monster re-awakens." James heaved a sigh and scribbled absentmindedly on the floor. He spoke to his chicken sketch. "In all my years with my parents, I have never seen them this nervous about a Mew threat before. Nor have I seen them leave Boston with the haste they did when your parents called the night you transformed."

"Our parents know each other?" Perry asked. That fact mildly surprised him.

"Uh-huh," James said, nodding to the same effect. "Since they were hatchlings.

"It might be nature's way of balancing good forces with evil forces. I don't know. I'm not sure. But it is said that the sea monster cannot be defeated except by the eagle. It is only a rumor actually, but most people are inclined to believe it. Especially since all the previous eagles eventually had to meet their sea monsters. Most died. But when they died, the sea monster just seemed to slither back into the depths of the sea."

"The ones that survived?" Sarah asked.

James shrugged. "Their bodies were never recovered. So not much can be said about them." James gazed at Perry for a while. Then, he said, "Your older brother, Richard's twin, was an eagle. He was killed before he could face the monster."

That one hit Perry in the face. He remained quiet. A hand rubbed his shoulder. He looked and saw it was Sarah's.

"My parents didn't tell me who killed him," James continued. "Just that when he died, the sea monster died with him. That's why I think you feel drawn to the sea monster. I think it's a test. A test to prove if you are really worthy of all the powers of an eagle. A test you may eventually need to pass because failure means death."

"So, I eventually face the sea monster?" Perry asked, his attention lost in the churning sea in the background. "And I will have to go to him."

"What?" James asked.

Perry didn't look at him. "I had a...vision of the monster. *It* said it wasn't going to come to me, that I was eventually going to come to him."

Sarah's voice interrupted his mesmerism with the sea. "Let's not jump to conclusion too quickly," she said. "There's still the clan general meeting tonight."

"Oh that," James said. "A necessary action to make official the choosing of the first option. That is, of course, if Greg Johnson can convince the assembly that the third option is the way to go. Unlikely, in the opinion of many."

"Wait, wait, wait," Perry said, flustered. "Start from the beginning. What are the three options?"

"Perry, tonight's meeting is going to be about choosing from three options," Sarah said to Perry, her eyes dark with the graveness of their discussion. "I've known about these three choices since yesterday. I just didn't know what they were. Obviously, Mr. James here does."

James smiled at Sarah. Then to Perry, his features filled with darkness. "Indeed, a decision will be made. One, kill the eagle Mew, and by so doing kill the sea monster. Two, task the eagle Mew with killing the monster, however unlikely it is for the eagle Mew to win. Three, create a special task force to seek and destroy the sea monster." He paused.

The silence stretched for sixty dreary, painful seconds. All the energy he had felt towards solving this sea monster mystery had evaporated. Now all he felt was a headache and a desire to go home to his bed.

"It's not spoken yet, but every Mew is leaning towards killing the eagle Mew," James added. He looked down. "From all indications, they might go that way."

"I bet it's because they want a piece of his eagle strength," Sarah added, angry.

"Could be," James said. "Greg Johnson is supposed to make a case for option three this evening. If he's successful, Perry will be safe."

"What's the likelihood of my father's success?" Perry asked, flashing James a hard look when he mentioned "my father." He didn't like hearing his father's name pronounced with such disrespect and flippancy.

"Not likely," James said.

Silence greeted James's response.

"I don't know what to do," Perry admitted after much contemplation. "I thought I could do this, but it's just too overwhelming. This connection...my connection with the sea monster. The general clan meeting's probable outcome. The threat to my life. I don't know..."

Sarah's hand was on his shoulder again. "Best thing is to do nothing, Perr," she said. "Let your parents handle it. Whatever happens tonight, we'll go from there."

"And if his father fails?" James was looking at Sarah, who frowned back at him. "I say we seek out the monster and kill it together. We can form our own task force, the three of us. Together, we can take down the monster." He said this with excitement in his voice. Perry wondered if he didn't fully understand the importance of his statement. James continued, "We sneak into the meeting this evening. We get enough information on the whereabouts of the creature. We go after it and kill it before others come after you and kill you."

"That sounds like a bad idea," Sarah said immediately, but said no more.

"It's the only idea that doesn't have me sitting idly by while my future is being planned," Perry said. "I've decided to make my own destiny and not have it rise and fall on other people's decision. If I'm going to die at the hands of another Mew or the sea monster, let it be on my own terms. Not others."

Both Sarah and James agreed to this.

"I'm going to that meeting," Perry said. "I want to know."

"Perry," Sarah said to him, concerned. "You know that you walking into a room full of agitated Mews is like lighting a fire in a room full of gasoline? The moment they find out who you are, you'll be dead."

"I'll take my chances," Perry said.

"I'm coming with you," James said. "Before you say no, I alone know the location of the meeting. It's not in Manhattan, for one. It's in Brooklyn. I know the exact location. You're going to need me."

Perry agreed.

"You need transport," Sarah said, "or at least money for transport. I'll provide the second."

Perry felt a warmth in his heart. He felt a bond develop between the three of them. They were willing to fight with him—to fight *for* him. This was more than he could ever have asked for.

"So how do we leave?" he asked James.

"We meet in the subway on East Forty-Second by eight this evening," James replied. "The meeting is going to be held in an abandoned warehouse somewhere on the outskirts of Brooklyn."

"All right," Sarah said, rising to her feet. James, then Perry, joined her.

Sarah looked west. Somewhere in that direction, their school stood. "I guess we fly home, then," she said. "My driver's probably come and gone."

"I think I'll—" Perry stopped as a strange feeling pulled his gaze to the water.

James was already bending to a crouch, probably to take off in bird form, when he hesitated and glanced at him. "What's wrong?"

Perry heard him and saw Sarah's sideways glance, but he didn't respond (or couldn't?). Rather, he started walking towards the water. He had his eyes to the horizon where the water had begun to churn and was steadily rising to a cyclone. It didn't take time for the winds to splash droplets of water on his face. Yet, he walked on.

"Perry!" Sarah screamed.

Perry kept walking, even when the waves lapped against his legs.

James ran to his side and wriggled his hand. "Perry, what are you doing?"

Perry wanted to reply, but he also wanted to get to that cyclone on the edge of the horizon. His desire to go swimming just simply overwhelmed his desire to answer James, so he ignored the boy and waded into the water.

Now Sarah was at his side and the hydro cyclone closed in. It was the sea monster; it was calling out to him. It was just a few yards away in the midst of the churning sea. If he could go a few more paces...

"Perry!" Sarah screamed again, desperation in her voice.

James glanced at the hydro cyclone. Beyond the spinning pillar of water, a giant serpentine-like creature wriggled softly, moving towards Perry as he wadded deeper into the river towards the creature.

They were already knee-deep in water when Perry faintly heard James say to Sarah, "It's the sea monster. It's controlling him. We have to get him out of the water!"

James grabbed ahold of Perry's hand with renewed vigor and yanked him backwards. Sarah did the same. Perry did not protest. They dragged his body out of the water. When they got to the beach they dragged him further away from the monster, which was now retreating to the horizon. The sand clung to their legs; it stuck to Perry's body like a second skin and prickled him. Once they were a good way from the sea, they dumped him on the floor, where he remained motionless until the irresistible pull left his mind.

Perry sat up and was instantly irritated by his soggy clothes and the innumerable tiny sand particles pinching him in several different places. He frowned up at Sarah and James who were looking down at him with worried eyes. "Ugh! I hate sand."

Sarah looked at James first.

James shrugged.

Sarah gazed back at him. "You kind of zoned out on us and went into the water."

Perry tried to get up. James helped him to his feet. "Yeah. That was weird."

"It was the sea monster." James brushed off the sand colony centered on his left cheek. "Since you're not yet ready to face it, don't go near water." He glanced back at the sea. It was as calm as it had been before the monster showed up. "You need to be more careful."

"What he needs is to go home," Sarah said with a concerned look.

"But why didn't it just kill us when we were in the water? Why doesn't it just attack us now?"

"That seems to be how it is, Perr," James replied. "It will not come to you because it knows that in the end, you will come to it." James took several steps away and crouched. "See you tonight." Then he leaped into the air. He transformed and rose with the wind, flying north.

"Bye, Perry," Sarah said. "Be careful, okay? Stay away from water. We'll figure this out together." She hugged him. Then, she turned and flew away. She headed first in the direction of the cliff. Perry saw her pick his bag and head back to him. She dropped it from her beak and he caught it. Then she flew back to the cliff, picked up her backpack, and flew higher and higher until she was lost in the iron-grey underside of the clouds.

Perry took his bag and trudged through the sand towards the cliff. One leap up the cliff as an eagle and he was on his way to his house. When he came through the mouth of the forest, the streets were already lit by streetlights. The school was locked and stood as a dark mass of brick and cement. Its street was even darker as the streetlights there had been broken by recalcitrant kids.

Perry got to the bus station and got on the next bus. The people stared at him, but he ignored them and found a lonely corner in the back. He sat there and sulked. Was this how he would defeat the sea monster? When it had such power over him? When it could take control of his body any time?

He shouldn't have lost control like that. He should have fought back. Perry struggled to resist the depression that was settling upon his heart. Was he good enough to save himself? Was his father's faith in him really warranted? He knew if he failed to protect himself or at least try to, it would prove that being average was just his lot in life. And one thing Perry understood well enough was that you couldn't cheat destiny.

Whatever happened in the end was what was meant to happen.

After Perry got to his stop, he walked the rest of the way to his house. Of course, his eyes were always searching. The skies first. Then the streets.

10
PERRY'S
NIGHT PLAN

erry saw Jake before Jake saw him.

Jake stood in the foyer of their apartment building, looking frustrated and flabbergasted. His brows were creased as he paced the floor, hands akimbo, looking out into the traffic. Every cab had him stopping for a second to check. When it wasn't Perry, he continued his pacing.

Perry approached him, veiled by the pedestrian traffic that followed on his path. Jake didn't see him because his attention was focused on the cars and the skies. It was already dark. The moon was already rising, and people passed by Jake oblivious to his plight.

Jake had his back to Perry when he finally got near enough. His first thought was to sneak by and enter the building. But he decided that it would be unfair to Jake since he had probably been waiting here for him for a long time.

"Perry!" Jake said, his tall figure towering over Perry. His momentary flush of happiness at seeing Perry was swallowed up by anger. "Where have you been?" he boomed. People stopped to look.

Perry tried to reply but was cut off by Jake.

Jake grabbed him by the hand and pulled him towards the door. "Never mind," he said, settling his emotions. He didn't seem to notice Perry's wet clothes.

Their climb to their apartment was silent. The apartment was even more silent. No one was around. The dishes were clean and arranged on the shelf. The dining room was spotless and showed no sign of use in the past hour. The usual chirpy voice of Lisa or Mother was missing, which made Perry sad. He felt their family was losing its vitality because of him. Now Lisa was off to some desert because it wasn't safe for her in New York City because of him. Oddly, the windows were boarded up.

Perry stood beside the dining table staring at the windows. Crusty old planks had been nailed to every windowsill, including the one in the living room. It wasn't an efficient boarding, but it would hold against an aerial assault, which was the reason, Perry surmised, Jake had boarded up the windows.

"Father gave the instruction," Jake said, following his gaze. "We won't be getting attacked by any birds tonight."

Perry's shoulders slumped. And it wasn't because his bag was heavy. His house had become a prison, all because of him.

"Go on," Jake said softly. "Go in and freshen up. I've ordered pizza."

Perry threw Jake a blank stare.

"What?" Jake shrugged. "That's all I can do. Now go to your room."

Perry strolled out of the dining room. The windows in his room were boarded up as well, though strays of night lights found their way into his room. Perry changed clothes after a thorough bath, which he needed to get all the sand off his body. Sometime during his shower, he heard the door open and Jake chat with the pizza delivery guy.

Once he was freshly clothed, he packed his bag again. He retrieved his transothe from where it was hidden in his vest and embedded it in his bag. If he carried it with him and Jake objected to his going to their neighbor's house for a sleepover, he didn't want to have incriminating evidence on him. He packed a blank book and a pen. He didn't yet know why he needed it.

"Perry," Jake hollered from outside. "Dinner's ready."

"Some dinner," Perry muttered, tightening the straps of his bag. "Coming," he yelled back.

Perry was nervous. Not just because he was going into the hornets' nest, but also because he didn't know if Jake would agree to let him go over to their neighbor's house. He sat down at the table with Jake, his anxiety weakening him. After three forced slices of pizza, he worked up the boldness to look up at Jake.

Jake smiled at him. "It's going to be all right, buddy," he said in a soft voice. "Nothing is going to get through that door or the windows."

Perry nodded and faced his food. It was going to be a lot harder than he had anticipated. Well, he could always go out through the window... then his head jerked to the boarded-up windows. *Oh no, I'm trapped!*

"Something wrong?" Jake asked, alert and searching the window.

Perry shook his head, pulling his gaze away from the boarded-up window. He glanced at the clock. The time said 6:30 PM. He had less than two hours to meet with Sarah and James at the train station. He shot to his feet.

Jake looked at his plate. "Aren't you going to finish that?"

"No," Perry replied, heading to his room. "I'm going to bed."

"Okay," Jake called back. "Just remember that that's all you get to eat today."

Perry shut the door and fell on his bed. He listened as Jake cleared the table, switched off all lights, and reclined on the couch in the living room. Perry fell in and out of uneasy sleep, waiting for Jake to doze off. He had flash dreams, nothing good. By twenty minutes past eight, there was no sound in the room except that of a reporter on the TV.

Perry crept out of bed. He gently slung his bag over his back and tiptoed out of the room. In the dining room, he could see Jake's flax hand over the couch's shoulder. He was asleep. Perry continued to the door and tried to open it.

The door was locked. His anxiety intensified.

He searched around for a key and found it lying in Jake's lap. He dropped his bag on the floor, taking care of every move he made. Jake lay on the couch slumbering. His red T-shirt had drool on it.

Perry let his hand hover above Jake's limp shape for a while before letting it descend to the key. As he touched the cold set, Jake woke.

Perry's first reaction was to jerk back. He was in the dining room when Jake's voice brought him to a halt.

Jake approached him, his visage that of fury. He looked first at the bag in Perry's hands; Perry didn't realize when he had picked up the bag. Then he looked at Perry.

"Do you not yet understand what kind of danger you are in?" Jake spoke with a reproving tone. "Where are you going to?"

Perry stuttered. "Next door. A sleepover."

Jake frowned. "What sleepover? You don't do sleepovers. Mother told me this specifically."

Perry dropped his head.

Jake yanked his bag out of his hands and said, "I'm going to ask you one more time." His tone had darkened. So had his face. "Where were you going to?"

Perry's bones trembled with fear. He tried to talk, but he was too scared to say anything.

Jake sighed. "Look, Perry," he said, "I understand how you feel. That need to fly. To be in the sky. It's something every normal hatchling experiences. But you're not just any normal hatchling. You're an eagle Mew. Your life will always be in danger if you do not learn to be strong. I'm going to have to hang on to this, buddy. Sorry."

Jake walked back into the sitting room, leaving Perry standing with a feeling of relief and distress. He found his way back to his bedroom and collapsed on the bed. The time said forty minutes past eight. He had to be at the train station in twenty minutes.

Perry jumped off the bed. He tried yanking the wood from the window and came off with a skin bruise in the process. He winced and stuck his finger in his mouth, soothing the injury with his tongue. His desperation grew with each passing second.

Perry paced in front of the bed, the steady drum of traffic a distraction. He watched time waste away, listening and hearing Jake's chuckle; sounds that indicated he was wide awake. Perry knew he was never getting out of the house now. Several minutes later, he snuck into the parlor. Jake was snoozing, but he had his bag and the bunch of keys in a tight grip. It was no use trying to retrieve any. It would only wake him and make him more aggravated.

Perry slugged back to his room. 9:00 PM. He tried harder to remove the boards from the window, but they wouldn't come unhinged. Perry fell on his bed for the umpteenth time, frustrated. Reality sunk in. He wasn't going to make it. He had been relegated to the background all his life. Why should now be different? Why should he get to have a say about anything? Whether he liked it or not, people were going to sit and decide if he lived or died.

Perry lay on his bed, feeling hurt and angry. Angry at himself. Angry at his parents. Angry at Jake and the whole world. He wished he hadn't been born. It was in this state that Perry fell into one of his horrid dreams.

A knock on the door woke him minutes later. Perry stirred on his bed, unaware of what had woken him. There was another knock somewhere. Perry became confused, though everything was still fuzzy. He hadn't locked the door, why would Jake need to knock? He trudged to the door and opened it, every muscle of his body begging for more rest. There was no one at the door. Perry frowned and shut it. He glanced at the clock; it said: 9:20 PM. James and Sarah were no doubt already on their way to Brooklyn.

There came another knock. It wasn't a knock per se, Perry realized. It was a peck on his window. His heart rose. He ran to the window.

"Who's there?" Perry said. Every sense in his body came alive. His fatigue was gone. There was a brief silence. He heard a swish, probably caused by transformation.

"Perr?" It was Sarah's voice.

Perry didn't think he could be this glad to hear her voice. "Yes?"

"James is at your door," Sarah said. "He's going to try and pick the lock."

"Pick the lock?" Perry said, surprised. He didn't know James could pick locks. But then again, he didn't know James that well.

"Yes, Perr, keep up," Sarah replied. "You need to make sure no one is around when he does. Knock three times when the coast is clear, and he'll pick the lock. Do you understand?"

"Yes," Perry replied. "Thanks, Sarah—"

There was another swish and a flap. Sarah was gone.

Perry listened for any sound in the front room. There was none. The TV was also silent. Perry crept into the dining room. Jake was fast asleep on the couch. He went over to assess the situation. His bag was trapped within Jake's bear hug. The keys were equally irretrievable. He stole out of the room. At the door, he knocked three times as Sarah had instructed him. A silence followed for up to a minute.

Jake twirled with a groan behind him.

Perry glanced over his shoulder. Jake settled in another position, the bag still encased in his bear hug.

"James?" Perry whispered at the door. "James, are you there?"

At first, there was no reply. Then, he heard the jangle of keys. "Be quiet, Perry Johnson," James replied. "This might take a while."

There was the sound of a key being inserted into the door. This was followed by the scratch of metal on metal as James worked the lock.

Perry settled on the floor, frozen in fear. If Jake awoke now, Perry would be in trouble.

"Where did you learn to pick locks?" Perry asked.

"You wouldn't believe me if I told you," James replied with a bit of a chuckle.

"Try me," Perry said. He leaned his back on the door so he could watch Jake.

"My parents taught me how to pick locks," James said.

"You're kidding, right?"

"Nah," James replied like it was normal for a parent to teach a twelve-year-old to break the law. "Remember I told you they are elite Mews? Well, it turns out that picking locks is part of an elite Mew's skill set. They're training me to work with them as an elite Mew. It's a family tradition." At the mention of tradition, the door came unlocked; Perry fell into the stairwell. James stood over him, looking sleek in his black leather jacket and black jeans.

James helped him up, gently shutting the door behind them.

"Glad to see you," James said, beaming and offering his hand.

Perry took it.

"We need to leave now," James said. He led the way down the stairs. "Otherwise, we'll miss the last train to Brooklyn."

They ran down the stairs and met Sarah in the foyer.

11

PERRY FLIES ACROSS NYC IN HUMAN FORM!

S arah was angry.

She stood looking at them, hands on her waist, face contorted into a frown. Perry stopped, startled, at the doorway for a moment, not sure what he had done wrong. Horn blasts from the road ahead pulled his attention to a classic black limousine trailing along the slow traffic. Perry already knew it would be a long night.

He approached Sarah. "What's the problem, Sarah?"

"Where have you been?" Sarah bellowed at him, shooting frightful glances his way.

Perry almost cringed away. If he had, it would have been embarrassing for him. People passed by them and paid no attention. Children's squabbling, they no doubt thought.

Perry first looked to his left and right, as if to get support from invincible beings. James was already ahead of them, looking in their direction. He didn't want to get involved.

"Uhm…" Perry stammered, "I was kinda held up by my brother?" He thought she already knew this. Wasn't that the reason they had come to rescue him?

"That's no excuse, Perr," Sarah countered. She wore a white jacket and a skimpy blue skirt. "You knew we needed to be at the train station by nine. Did you think your brother would have allowed you to waltz out of the house? Have you not learned anything?"

That hurt Perry, bad. Maybe he should have been more cautious in planning his escape before nine. Maybe he should have thought about interference from his family. Maybe he should have put into consideration the danger surrounding his life, but that gave Sarah no right to talk to him that way. He was happy she was with them, though. However, he knew that there was something else besides his lateness. There was something bothering her. A little complication that must have developed. Again, Perry was ignorant.

"What's the matter, Sarah?"

Sarah growled and started in James's direction. Perry fell into line with the duo and they hurried along the traffic.

"The assembly would have gathered by the time we get there. It will be impossible to get in then," Sarah said, waving her hand at the traffic as they strolled along the sidewalk.

"What?" Perry came to a halt.

A tall lady in a red dress stumbled into him. Hissing, she continued on her way. She looked over her shoulder, flashed him an evil look, and turned a corner.

When he calmed his heart, both Sarah and James were looking into his face.

"I'd hoped that if we got there before the meeting began, we could sneak in amidst the uproar," James said. "But now we are late and security around the facility will be tight. We might not be able to make it in."

Sarah was still frowning. Not at him, but at their precarious situation.

Perry felt cold, and it was not because of the frigid blast around them. Unknown to him, his breathing was running out of control. In fact, everything was running out of his control. He couldn't even make it to a meeting early. Now his chances of getting to know his enemy were nil.

"And that's not all. There have been more deaths. It's gone from bad to worse, Perry. The sea monster is rampaging up and down the eastern sea board, and the Mews are doing all they can to prevent humans from getting caught in its rage. Nerves are frayed. People are scared out of their minds. It might not go in your favor tonight." James had a mournful look on his face.

Sarah touched him lightly on the shoulder, bringing his watery gaze to her face. She smiled warmly and said, "There's still a chance, Perr. Let's not lose hope too soon. Tell him, James."

James turned from Sarah to Perry. "It would be unwise to return to our houses now after the effort it took us to sneak out. We might as well check out the facility. There might be a way to get in. Right? Who knows? And your Father can make a strong case for you that will get accepted."

"Come on," Sarah said, pulling him.

They crossed the road and continued down the avenue. James flagged down a yellow cab. It seemed to stop and veer towards the curb. But when he, a bearded Arab man, saw the trio, he veered away and drove off. Every cab driver they tried to flag down drove away when they saw them.

"Who would want to pick a bunch of kids at ten at night, huh?" Sarah puffed, exasperated. She spun around on her heels, looking up at the lamp-post and growling aloud. "Why can't things just go our way? For once?"

They were on Third Avenue now. The traffic was light, both cars and people. They had been walking for several minutes. Perry's ankles were aching. He needed to rest for a while. He looked around and the gutter ledge called to him.

James yelled, waving his hands at an oncoming vehicle. The cab slowed with a sharp screech that had the two boys jerking deeper into the curb. The mad driver came to a halt and leaned towards them. "Where ya going, kids?" The young driver didn't look like he had shaved in three days. He wore night robes, a crooked smile plastered on his face.

Red flags arose in Perry's mind. James glanced at him. The look on James's face told Perry that James too had a bad feeling about the driver. Sarah came up beside Perry, looking into the cab.

"This doesn't look good," she whispered.

"We have no choice," James replied. "No other driver will take us."

"So what, we risk our lives with a driver that's probably sleep driving?"

James furrowed a brow and took one more look at the driver. He had a crust of chips on his left lips. He had a dreamy expression in his eyes, and he held the crooked smile like he had a stroke. "We can Mew up if he attacks us."

Sarah grunted and shot James a glare. "Mew up? Really?"

"Kids, are you coming or not?" the man said, relaxing back in the driver's seat and gripping the steering wheel tight. He revved the engine.

"It's your decision, Perr," Sarah said. "But I think it's a bad idea."

Perry looked at James.

"It's our best option now, given that we're already late," James said.

"The train station," Perry said to the cabbie and opened the door. They trooped into the unsanitary back of the cab and the cab driver stomped the gas pedal. They were thrown against the seat.

They screamed all the way.

The driver never relented on the gas pedal. He preferred rather to swerve sharply than to slow down. They must have caused several accidents on the road. The only thing that slowed the maniac was the gridlock in traffic that they encountered several blocks from the train station.

"We can't stay here," Sarah said. She pulled out a hundred-dollar bill and gave it to the driver.

They pushed out of the vehicle, leaving the driver shocked. He followed them with his gaze as they ran down the sidewalk. The street was alive with college students and couples. The blast of horns, the revs of engines, the cheerful laughter of college girls all melted to the back of Perry's mind as his only focus was getting to the meeting.

"Perry!" Sarah grabbed his shoulder and forced him to stop.

"What is it?" Perry panted heavily.

"We have to fly," James said, chest heaving. He was sweating profusely. "We can't make the 10 PM train on foot."

"It's dark and it's only for a few minutes," Sarah continued. "Nothing could go wrong."

"Okay," Perry whispered. He was more than happy to oblige his unceasing desire for the skies.

"Look," Sarah said, pointing to an alleyway in the distance. "We can transform there."

They ran for the opening in the sidewalk, the parting in the line of skyscrapers. Perry stumbled in first, then the others. The alley was dark and damp. Wrangled dumpsters littered the corners. Spilled, marshy garbage carpeted the floor. In the deep, a figure stirred. It was the figure of a man crouching against the wall.

"We should leave," Sarah whispered in fear. She started the retreat, but nobody followed.

"There isn't another suitable alleyway where we can change for two more blocks," Perry said, stepping forward to intercept the man. "I'll handle this."

Perry closed in on the homeless man. The man growled and sprung at him with fingers shaped as claws. Perry was the one with real claws. He spread his hands and summoned the eagle.

Nothing happened.

The man grabbed his neck in a grip hold. Perry choked.

Sarah screamed.

There was a transformation followed by flaps.

Perry felt the wind on his back and felt the man's grip loosen on his neck. He fell to his knees, struggling to breathe. The man retreated, scared, into the alleyway, stumbling over garbage cans and making a ruckus.

The winds ceased and Sarah and James were humans once more, standing at his side. Perry stood.

"What happened?" James asked.

"Do you have your transothe?" This came from Sarah.

"My trans..." Perry searched his clothes. Then, he remembered he had left it in his bag. Jake had his bag. "At home?"

"You can't transform without your transothe, Perr," Sarah said. "Didn't anybody tell you that?"

Perry shook his head. If he couldn't transform, then he couldn't be of much use. He couldn't make it to the train station in time. Game over.

"We have to carry you, Perry," James said. "It's the only way. We're out of time."

Sarah frowned. "Have you lost it? You want to get Perry killed?"

"I'll do it," Perry said immediately.

"Absolutely not!" Sarah said, stomping her feet and folding her arms. "I'm not carrying you, Perr. I'm not going to be responsible when you fall on your back and have to be in a wheelchair the rest of your life."

"Sarah," Perry said. "Please."

Sarah looked away, silent.

James glanced at his watch. "We don't have much time, Perry. We have to go now."

Perry grabbed Sarah with a new desperation. "Sarah, I beg you. Don't fail me now."

She ignored him. He shook her vigorously.

"All right, all right," Sarah said through clenched teeth, pushing Perry's hands off her shoulders. "But we fly high," she said. "So if you slip, we have enough time to catch you."

"We fly high anyway," James replied.

James and Sarah transformed. They clamped tight onto Perry's shoulders, their claws digging into his skin, and lifted him into the air. Perry ignored the sharp pain in his shoulders where he hung from the birds. His head spun as they shot up into the dark skies; it was the same feeling he got when he was in an elevator. When they were high enough so that no human could possibly make out Perry and the birds, they soared towards the train station.

Perry hollered, excited, as the air rushed through his hair, face, and clothes. He was scared out of his wits because he knew if he fell, he was dead. Notwithstanding, he felt exhilarated. New York night life was under his feet. The whole world was under his feet. He zipped, legs wriggling behind him, towards the train station thanks to the falcon on his left shoulder and the owl on his right shoulder.

They slowed as the train station came into view. They fell towards the ground at the same speed as they had when they shot up to the clouds;

they had to protect the existence of Mews. Perry's feet touched the ground in seconds. He didn't stay standing for long. He hit the floor, his head spinning in revolt.

James and Sarah transformed back.

Perry was a little happy to see that they stumbled and fell, too, when they transformed. He wasn't the only person having troubles with bird to human conversions. James ran out the alley while Sarah crouched at his side. She helped him to his feet.

They staggered into the subway station and waited for James at the platform. The clock said ten minutes past ten and the platform was deserted.

Perry still held on to Sarah. "It's past ten, Sarah. The train has left. We failed."

Sarah looked at him but said nothing. There was nothing to say. He was probably right.

James ran down the stairs, jumped onto the platform, and ran towards them. He was holding three tickets. Before he spoke, Perry heard the faint sound of blaring horns. He felt the ground tremble. A train was approaching.

James was beaming. "The train got delayed at Queens," he said, catching his breath. He handed out the tickets. "We're lucky."

Perry flushed with relief. He stood on his own when the train stopped before them. The doors parted for them to enter, and they closed when Perry and his friends were seated. The car was empty, except for a figure lying at the back. The figure was cloaked in a black robe.

As soon as the train began towards Brooklyn, Perry exhaled and allowed himself to savor their little victory. However, two simple questions nagged at the back of his mind. One, how would they get into the meeting? Two, if things went south, how would he escape since he couldn't transform? The night was definitely going to be a long one.

12
THAT'S ONE SCARY WOMAN

erry saw trouble when he saw the burly teenager with the bloody nose. They were a rowdy bunch, five of them, each sporting a symbol of their penchant for violence: a bruise, a gash cut, blood-stained sweaters. One had a broken hand in a dirty cast. They entered the car from one end, talking or rather shouting. Sarah huddled closer to Perry, gripping his arm.

"We'll be lucky if they leave us alone," she whispered into his ear. She was looking at the approaching pack.

"It helps not to look at them." Perry tilted his eyes to the window to gaze out at the dark countryside while keeping the teenagers in his periphery and observing them. "Pretend you're not here."

Perry glanced at James for a moment and saw that the boy was looking at the dangerous boys. There was a dangerous look on his face. With that look, James was inviting trouble. What was his problem? Perry thought. James seemed to have an unhealthy proclivity for excitement. That wasn't Perry's style at all. He preferred life to be quiet where he could be alone, in the corner, safe, where nobody could see him or disturb him. Perry tried to warn James, but before he could tell him to back down, the boy with the gash across the face noticed them and flashed them a cruel smile.

"What do we have here?!" he roared, bringing the attention of the occupants of the train car—which were five murderous looking bullies and a sleeping figure in the back—onto them. The boys laughed out at the jeer of their leader, calling them names like suckers, lost souls, and the likes.

"Oh boy, are we going to get it," Sarah whispered as the teenagers neared them.

"Don't worry, I've got this." James kept up his unflinching façade.

"You've got this?" Perry whispered back in anger. "You created this mess!"

"How?" James turned to Perry as if he had insulted him.

"The way you looked at them, James. You invited their trouble."

James face twisted into a confused look. "What would you rather have me do, Perry? Look afraid? Cower back? I'm going to be an elite Mew, Perry. Elite Mews don't back down or cower from anything or anyone."

"Yeah, but you're not an elite Mew yet," Sarah said.

From the stunned look on James's face, Perry saw that Sarah's comment had hit home with James.

"What are you three talking about?" The boy with the gash loomed over them. The fetid breath was so close that Perry, James, and Sarah jerked out of the seat and onto the aisle. They were blocked on both sides. The trio huddled close together, hands brushing hands, hearts racing.

The gashed-up boy remained kneeling on the seat before them and kept on talking, seemingly oblivious to their fright. "You insulting us in our presence?" he questioned them, a suspicious look that could easily lead to anger appearing on his face.

The boys with him let out a theatric gasp like it was taboo to insult their leader.

"Dagger!" the boy called, walking past the two that blocked the trio in the front.

The boy with the cast around his hand answered. "Yes, Machete?"

"Tell them what we do to people who talk about us behind our backs," Machete said.

The boy cast a horrendous smile over them, revealing crooked, scanty teeth. "We chop them into tiny little pieces and dump them in the Hudson."

Perry's fear skyrocketed. With all that's going on with the threat on his life, he never thought he would die at the hands of dumb teenagers in an empty train car. He glanced at Sarah. Her eyes were wide with terror. James, however, seemed unfazed. Perry wondered if the guy had a plan. They couldn't transform here. The space was too tight. Perhaps, they could not really judge the teenagers' response to their bird form. Would it be fear or interest? People who bore outrageous names such as Dagger and Machete couldn't be trusted to reason sanely.

Machete closed the distance between them. Perry guided Sarah behind him. His vantage point put him in close proximity to the diagonal gash that stretched from Machete's right temple to left cheek. The groove had along its length, in a copious quantity, red crusts like spices on a pizza. The boy reeked. Of the sewer, booze, blood, *and who knows what else?*

"I'm so going to love this," the boy said with a serious look and the hint of satisfaction in his voice.

Perry saw that he couldn't have been older than eighteen. He also saw that he was a sadist. There was no reasoning with sadists. Perry didn't see a way out. They couldn't fight. They couldn't run. They were doomed.

Machete retreated a yard away and said, "Search them. Take away every valuable. Wouldn't want to damage the goods while we take care of this bunch."

Before the first boy could approach, James stepped up to Machete. "Look, pal," he said. "You don't want to do this. Let us go and we promise our parents won't hunt you down and kill you."

Machete's response was swift. His hands went up in a heartbeat and struck out against James. James raised his hands to block. The palm slapped his arm and he stumbled back falling against Perry. Perry held him from crashing to the ground. Machete lunged for James faster than Perry could process thought.

He grabbed James from Perry's hands, shoving Perry against Sarah. Perry slammed into Sarah, knocking her to the ground with a yelp. Machete rumbled in anger, lifting James up as though he weighed as little as a sheet of paper. "You dare speak to me like that?!"

James wriggled, kicking his legs against Machete's shin.

Machete raised his hands one more time. At that close range, Perry knew James would be knocked unconscious.

"You will not hit that boy again!" A voice bellowed from behind. It belonged to a woman. Every head turned just in time to see a huge woman arise from underneath a black cloak in the back of the car. Her skin and eyes were as black as midnight. Her voice was powerful and strong. The woman's scattered hair scraped the car's ceiling as she towered over them. The teens were like ants before the woman. The boys standing between Perry and the woman scurried past them to stay behind their leader.

Machete dropped James, who scampered away from the gang leader and rejoined Sarah and Perry. He was trembling with fear and sobbing.

"Mind your own business, you big fat oaf!" Machete called.

The woman frowned and took three quick steps towards the boys. Their bravado fell that instant. They spun on their heels and bolted, fumbling out of the car like frightened children.

The woman knelt before Perry, James, and Sarah, a warm motherly look on her face. "Hi," she said. "My name is Judith. I'm not going to hurt you. I have a son just like him." She motioned to James, who was still a little rattled from his experience.

"Hi," Perry said. "I'm Perry. This is James and that's Sarah."

"Hi," Sarah said.

"Where's your stop?" asked Judith.

"Brooklyn," Perry said, helping Sarah to her feet. He turned to help James up.

"That's good," the woman said, rising to her full stature. "Those cruel boys will not be disturbing you again." Then the woman looked confused. She eyed them suspiciously. "What are you kids doing outside of the house at this time?" She looked to Perry for an answer.

Perry looked first at the woman then looked away. He knew he had to lie. If he didn't, the woman would bundle them to the nearest police station. But he struggled to speak the deceitful words. Maybe it was because the woman reminded him so much of his controlling mother.

"Sorry, ma'am," James said, smoothly covering Perry's lack of words. "We are actually on our way home." James feigned fatigue, sighing. "Late night party. Our parents are expecting us within the hour."

Judith eyed James for one long minute, then nodded. "Okay. Be safe." The woman turned and trudged back to her seat in the back. Then she laid her huge form on the seat and covered it with the black coat.

"What is wrong with you?" James frowned at Perry. "You want to get us caught?"

Perry remained silent, walked away, and sat on their chair.

"He doesn't lie," Sarah whispered to James.

"He doesn't?" James replied. "Oh..."

Sarah came and sat beside him, while James sat in the chair opposite theirs. They weren't seated for long before the train ground to a halt in Brooklyn. They hopped out of the train and dashed out of the train station. James led the race. They ran until they entered a residential area.

"Wait!" Sarah put her hands on her knees and gasped for breath. "I need to stop for a minute."

Perry was gasping, too, but he was glad he hadn't been the one to stop first.

James pretended not to be exhausted. "Well, we're close to the warehouse now so it's good to slow down."

"There's a lot of Mew activity here," Perry said.

James answered. "Yeah."

The area was quiet and dark except for the soft lights from the houses. The roads were empty except for one person strolling here and there. Perry and Sarah followed James down a street that had a bush on one side and a line of houses on the other. High above, they saw Mew-sized birds in the tens, patrolling.

"They won't attack us," James said as they strolled along.

Perry gave him a doubtful look.

James motioned for the skies. "They are here to scan for trouble. The other kind of trouble."

"What other kind of trouble?" Perry asked.

"Evil nature," Sarah said in a low tone.

Perry remembered Richard's explanation of nature's split personality disorder and nodded.

They got to an area where the streets were increasingly narrow, and the houses clustered tightly together. That's when they saw the Mews in their terrestrial forms. Giant leopards, tigers and grizzly bears lurked in the shadows away from human sight—searching for threats. Perry couldn't deny he was scared. They kept on the major streets, walking beside strolling couples whenever they could.

But then, a huge tiger blocked their way.

James whispered, "That's one of my parents' friends."

"Some friend," Perry whispered back.

The creature soon had them pinned in the backyard of a house, away from the streets, away from human intervention.

"It's all right, guys," James said to them. "It's a friend of my dad's."

James looked at the white monstrosity. "It's okay, Joe," he said to the tiger. "Dad knows we are here." He paused as if listening to the tiger. The tiger never spoke a word. Rather, it growled with a furious look, it's white razor-sharp teeth sending shivers through Perry's body.

"Of course," James said after a while. "You could confirm with him later, but we have to go. We are visiting a friend around these parts."

He paused again. They were no doubt communicating on some level of relationship. Perry couldn't tell which.

"No," James said, shaking his head with a slight smile. "This isn't one of my elaborate charades. See who that is?" James pointed at Sarah. Sarah took a step closer to Perry. "That's a Croft."

Another pause. The tiger growled all the way, drooling on the green grass.

"Yes, Joe," James said with a tone of exasperation. "She's also visiting a friend with me."

Perry didn't think Joe was a smart person.

The tiger turned and sprang away.

"Be safe too, Joe," James called after the Mew before it disappeared around the corner of the house.

"What was that all about?" Sarah asked when they were back on the road. Down the street, they saw an abandoned train yard.

"Joe is a member of my clan," he replied, leading them through rusty gates into the train yard. The ground was peppered with granite. James chose a path through the farm of corroded train cars towards a fence in the distance. "He's a sworn protector of my parents. He's like my uncle."

"Is it still safe for us to continue?" Perry said. "Don't you think he might alert your parents and mine of our coming?"

"Perry, if you're getting cold feet now, we could leave," James replied with a brief look his way.

"No," Perry replied. "I just don't want anything to compromise our mission."

"Joe is definitely going to alert my parents," James replied. "However, he can't because he can't abandon his post. *Unless* he's summoned back to the warehouse by my parents who happen to be in charge of securing this gathering."

"What are the chances that he gets summoned back to the warehouse?"

"High," James said. "But probably not before we get into the warehouse." James paused at the metal interlocking fence and gazed at the large barn. The huge double doors in the front were locked and guarded by two Mews in human form. The only side door on the left, near the end of the long building, was guarded by a large fat Mew. In the skies, Mew birds roamed. The session had begun.

"We're too late," Sarah said, clinging to the fence and falling gently to the granite floor. James joined her on the ground, his gaze fixed on the building.

"There's no way we are getting into that building. Not without alerting hundreds of Mews to our presence."

Perry searched the fence and saw a cut in the metal, through which they could slither into the road that separated the train yard from the warehouse's fenceless compound. He fell to his hands and knees, crawled to the opening, and slithered carefully through the fence. He gave way for his friends but remained on his knees. Any sudden movements could attract the attention of the two elite Mews at the door.

"This is stupid, Perr," Sarah said, coming up beside him. "We can't get in. At least we tried. If they catch you, they might kill you, seeing as you're the eagle."

"Listen to her, Perry," James said, once through the fence. "Elite Mews don't fail. They *will* catch you."

"You said elite Mews don't leave their posts," Perry said, taking note of the brown transothe that hung from the waist of one of the Mews at the door. "That means they won't run after us when they see us dashing towards the side door."

"Yeah?" James said. "But they will alert other elite Mews."

"Not when they see you waving at them," Perry replied. "No offense, James, but it seems you have a reputation for being a thrill seeker. They'd rather let the fat man guarding the door take care of us rather than bring down the whole force of the elite Mews on three misguided hatchlings."

True," Sarah said. "But how do we get past the fat man?"

"We run past him and hope he doesn't follow us." Perry sprung to his feet before they could respond. He made a mad dash for the warehouse.

13

THE GENERAL CLAN MEETING

P erry almost got run over by a bus. He'd jumped the slope of granite that connected the fence to the highway and continued into the road without looking. The vehicle had no lights on and swerved to avoid hitting him. Perry fell to his knees, his heart pounding. The others knelt beside him.

"You want to get yourself killed?" Sarah gasped, but he ignored her. He was assessing the elite Mews in front of the warehouse. They hadn't seen them yet, because they had been distracted by the stupid driver who didn't have enough sense to drive with his headlights on. James began to say something too, but Perry's gaze was fixed on the warehouse. The moment the two elite Mews weren't looking, Perry sprung to his feet and raced for the warehouse, angling towards the side of the building.

"Hey!" one of the two said.

James waved his hands at them, racing alongside Perry. "It's all right, Tess, I want to see my dad!" he yelled.

They didn't pursue.

Perry slowed and pushed into the rough wood of the warehouse's outside wall, inching further towards the side entrance. The fat man hadn't seen them yet. James and Sarah followed beside him, trying as much as possible to reduce the distinction between themselves and the wall. There was no light around. The moon was hidden behind thick dark clouds. So, the eyes could be easily fooled.

"Darn kid," Perry heard Tess say. "I don't know whether to think him foolish or brave." The other one with her gave a grunt. No more was said.

The chubby man, whose torso was bare and who wore a baggy brown pair of pants, filled the open doorway, looking up and around vigilantly.

"All right, Brainiac," Sarah said. "What next?"

Perry looked at them. "We need a distraction."

Sarah rolled her eyes. "You mean you want one of us to sacrifice ourselves? I thought we were in this together."

James's eyes looked beyond Perry's and he said, "That might not be necessary." He motioned to a point behind Perry.

Perry looked back and saw that the guard was now talking to someone inside the warehouse. Before long, the man left the doorway and headed towards the edge of the empty field of grass beside the warehouse. Another person, a slim, fully clothed guy, joined him and together they lit a cigarette.

James let loose a silent horrified gasp. "That's against elite Mews' regulation."

Perry sneaked up along the wall until they were behind the men. But neither of them turned. They kept on blowing rings of white smoke into the air.

Perry, James, and Sarah entered a narrow corridor lit only by dim service lights. There were open doors along the walls, doors that led into office spaces no doubt. From these doors, silent, clipped conversations escaped into Perry's ears. Perry couldn't tell if they were elite Mews or not. He was already enthralled by the noise he heard coming from the brown door at the end of the corridor. It was the door that led to the main floor of the warehouse.

They dashed in the direction of the door. Perry pushed the cold metal door and they slipped in, coming into a massive room brimming with people.

The uproar was deafening. Everyone talked at the same time. No voice was distinct. Some people shouted insults. No one paid them any attention as they made their way through the raucous gathering. The crowd's attention was directed at someone in the front of the warehouse. Perry and his friends kept their heads down and pushed through the mob towards the back of the room. Once there, they gathered in a huddle.

"This is such a bad idea," Sarah said, her voice embroiled in fear.

Perry was crazy scared. The people that surrounded him were a kaleidoscopic cross from all walks of life. From brutish looking men with fierce eyes that spoke of terror unimaginable, to business men and women with suits and hand bags. From college students with jeans and polo shirt to middle-class housewives. They all joined in a melodious outcry, demanding the death of the eagle hatchling—*his* death.

Unknown to Perry, his eyes had begun to water. All these people wanted his death. All sincere-looking people whose only fear was the monster his hatching had resurrected. Perry decided it was a bad idea to have come here. There was no pacifying this crowd. There was nothing his parents could say or do to make them spare him.

"Perr," Sarah said, rubbing his back. Her show of affection only made it worse for him. He began to sob. He hid this from them, shrugged her hands off his shoulder, and said, "I'm fine."

Sarah eyed him. Perry knew there was no deceiving her. She no doubt knew that his heart burned with hurt. She gave him a humorless smile.

James, who was folding his arms beside them, leaned in closer. "Your father is up," he whispered. Just then, the crowd got quiet.

Mounting the distant podium were five figures. Mother, Father, Richard, and two people Perry did not know: a fierce looking man and a woman with feisty eyes. They had an uncanny resemblance to James.

Sarah whistled softly. "The Fortins," she whispered.

"Yeap," James quipped. "My parents." He didn't seem overly happy to see them.

The warehouse was large and filled with hundreds of people, however, in the quietude that attended the presence on the stage, Perry's father's voice carried far.

"You know what I'm here for, so I will not attempt to waste your time," Greg said. He spoke with a voice that carried no appeal. He spoke with an edge in his voice like he was about to issue a threat. He spoke with a deadly determination that kept everyone transfixed on his speech. He was not there to beg; he was there to make them see reason.

"There are three options that have been brought before you this night concerning the new sea monster threat. One, kill the eagle hatchling. Two, task the eagle Mew with killing the monster. Three, set up a task force that will attempt to kill the monster."

"We already know which option we want," shouted one from the crowd.

"Kill the eagle hatchling!" said another.

"Or send him to fight the monster!" cried yet another.

Everyone began to yell at the same time.

Father glanced at Mr. Fortin, who gave him a reassuring look.

"Listen to me!" Father shouted. The place calmed.

"As everyone already knows, the eagle hatchling is my son. So if you think you can kill him without a fight, you're wrong. And believe me, you will get the fight of your life." The silence was knife sharp. "Let's set up a task force. The Fortins have agreed to head the force. I, Joanna, and Richard will be in the task force as well as the elite Mews' finest." Father's voice reduced to a whisper that Perry could barely hear. "We can fight this monster. We can kill it. We don't have to lose our souls by killing a child."

Perry thought they were going to accept his Father's offer. He hoped they would. That's why he stood there, holding his breath, waiting for the silence to end. He did not yet take note of the suspicious look two men, who seemed to be conspiring with each other, were giving him.

James grabbed his shirt. "We've got to go."

Perry slapped off his hands. "I have to hear the verdict."

Just like that, the silence gave way to an outcry. "Kill the eagle!"

"You can't. We have to go now," James said, nodding towards a group of five people who sported red outfits. "The Red Tails. They've spotted us."

Perry's heart skipped a beat. He glanced at the group. They wore red tops and black pants. They were looking in his direction, their eyes full of malice for him. Perry turned to James. "You mean the red-tailed kites?"

James nodded, visibly terrified. "The ones that attacked you on your way from Nevada. Yes, I heard. You killed one of their own. Now, they want your head." James grabbed Perry and pulled him towards the door. Perry got a hold of Sarah's hands, pulling her, too.

"But it was an accident," Perry complained. He had not meant to kill the kite; he had only meant to scare it. But it had turned out wrong. Just like this little expedition of theirs was about to turn out wrong.

"Doesn't matter now," James said, sandwiched between bodies. "These Red Tails are vengeful creatures. All they know is you killed one of their own. That's enough for them to want to kill you back."

Perry looked over his shoulder past Sarah and saw that the Red Tails were following cautiously from behind. Perry's heart began to race. A fight was brewing. They couldn't get away alive without fighting. Perry didn't have his transothe. Those kites were going to tear him apart and it wasn't because he was a Mew energy booster. Even if he hadn't turned into an eagle, he would still have managed to botch things up and given every Mew in the country a reason to hate him and want to kill him.

It was an accident! After all, didn't they attack first?

The Red Tails seemed to want to kill him without interference from other Mews. Otherwise, they would have alerted other Mews to his presence. He was, after all, the reason for this meeting. They wanted him for themselves, which was good and bad for him.

They pushed through the door and zipped down the hallway. There were people there. The three wove around them and continued down the corridor. The door behind the people burst open as the Red Tails poured into the corridor behind them. They shouted for them to stop or be stopped. The fat man turned, startled at first. But before he could regain his composure and understand what was happening, they zipped past him into the open.

Perry turned and raced towards the main road.

James and Sarah came up beside him. Behind them, the Reds bounded into the open. Three transformed and took to the skies, no doubt preparing for an attack dive, while the other two closed the distance between them.

"We can't make it on foot," Sarah panted. "We have to fly."

"Don't you think I know that?" Perry snapped at her. He regretted it immediately, seeing the shock give way to hurt in her eyes. But he didn't have the time to think about her feelings.

James broke from them once they cleared the side of the building. "You guys continue. I'll be with you shortly!"

"Where are you going to?" Perry was flustered. Things were falling apart too fast.

"We can't make it back to the train by ourselves. We need help!" James replied, not turning back.

Sarah slowed, but Perry grabbed her jacket and pulled her along. They crossed the road, climbed the slope, and slithered through the cut in the fence. Perry turned. James was running away from the warehouse towards them. The Reds were nowhere to be found.

"Here, take this," James said when he was through the fence, handing him a brown transothe.

Perry took the material. He closed his eyes and felt the rush of power within him.

"Where did you get that?" Sarah asked.

"The female Mew at the door," James said with a smile. "She doesn't really need a transothe."

Perry nodded, eyes widened, dead serious. They weren't out of the woods yet.

"We need to keep moving," James said, rose to a crouch, and made his way towards the other side of the train yard.

"What is it, James?" Perry said, keeping low, and following. "What's wrong?"

James ignored him. He crouched at the gate.

"Why are we stopping?" asked Sarah.

Perry caught a movement up. A bird descended from the sky; a big black vulture. It transformed before touching the ground so that it was a tall man wearing a black robe. Perry recognized Mr. Monte, the Messenger Vulture. *What is he doing here?* Perry thought.

Mr. Monte pulled James up roughly and whispered to him. "It's still too dangerous, but it's the best we can do at this time. Do you understand?"

James nodded.

"Get him to the train and get him out of here. It's no longer safe. If he dies, it's on you." Mr. Monte threw James back to the ground like he was a noisome nuisance. Without so much as a glance of recognition towards Perry, Mr. Monte turned and took to the skies, transforming into his aerial form with a simple flap of his hands.

"What was that all about?" Sarah asked. She and Perry helped him to his feet.

James turned to them. He looked afraid. "We are under attack."

"Yeah, James," Perry replied. "We know that already. Why was Mr. Monte here? What was he talking about?"

"No, you don't understand," James replied. "We are under attack from evil nature. It's never happened like this before. Not this magnitude." He then turned and ran into the street. They followed him.

14

A CERTAIN MANSION ON A CERTAIN STREET IN BROOKLYN

They ran down the deserted street in silence.

It was dead and dark. There were no Mews in sight, both terrestrial and aerial, and Perry was beginning to feel an uneasy gloom descend upon him. Perry searched the skies, ceaselessly and unsettled, but there was no sign of any Red Tail or even a normal bird. Dark clouds, stretching the length and breadth of the heavens: this was all he saw. It was as if the firmaments had prepared to mask a great bloodshed. The moon, in lieu with this great conspiracy, had allowed itself to be veiled; not even a shred of luminescence escaped the great hiding.

Perry was now deep in fear. He didn't want to die. Of course, he was only twelve. He didn't want his friends to die either, at least not because of him. They should never have come to this clan meeting. If they hadn't, they wouldn't have to be running for their lives.

James, who was one step ahead of them, paused, raising his hands and signaling for them to stop. They stopped behind him in the middle of the road, spotlighted by a street light above. Perry noticed the steady rise and fall of James's chest, which told him that the thrill seeker was terrified. *Of what?* Perry wondered. *What could have made this guy so afraid?* James must know something. Perry was bent on finding out what James knew.

James gazed down the empty road with squinted eyes. Perry followed his gaze. They were back where they had met the tiger, houses on one side and bushes on the other. The area was silent and the houses dark, as if everybody in these houses were deceased. In the distance, the street fed into another road. Perry knew James couldn't see that far, but even if he could see that far, there wasn't a person in sight. So why was James looking so intently at nothing?

Perry glanced at Sarah. She looked bored and unconcerned.

"James?"

James flinched a bit. He turned and, for a moment, blinked at Perry as though he was surprised at Perry's presence. Then, he raised his eyebrow in realization. "What?"

"Why are we standing here?" Perry asked. "We are close to the train station."

"We have to hide," James said, ignoring Perry's question.

"Why?" Sarah was irritated. "There's no one here."

James ignored her question. He ambled off the street and crouched at the corner of a house.

Perry and Sarah exchanged curious looks before walking into the shadow of the house where James was. They knelt beside him.

Perry said in a low tone, "James, what is it?" James was obviously in shock.

James swallowed. His eyes fluttered for a moment. "We're all going to die. And it's on me."

Perry didn't know why he did so, but when James spoke, he looked instinctively at Sarah. Her eyes widened. It was her first real demonstration of fear since they had left the house. Sarah's eyes sort of glazed over as they sought Perry's. When she saw he was already looking at her, she frowned and looked away. She was still mad at him for snapping back at her earlier. He would have to apologize to her. Later. Now, they were about to die.

"We are not going to die tonight, James," Perry said with real conviction. "Nothing is on you. We chose to come here. It was our decision, not yours."

James smiled. It was a smile of sarcasm. "You don't understand, Perry Johnson—"

"Well, then make me understand," Perry snapped. "Why are we crouched here in the dark when the train station is close by?"

James remained quiet. He closed his eyes for a long minute. When he opened them, he said, "The train that's going to take us to Manhattan is still on the way. If we wait at the train station, we'll be mugged by the Red Tails." He looked into Perry's eyes. "You won't survive. But Perry, you must survive. For the sake of us all."

"What's that supposed to mean?" Sarah said, her voice a little guarded.

James turned so he faced him and Sarah. "Perry's eagle didn't just re-awaken the sea monster. For some reason, evil nature is becoming stronger."

"And you know this how?" Sarah said.

"You know how good nature is the dominant form and that evil nature spawns monsters here and there?"

Sarah nodded.

"How many of these monsters are usually spawned?"

"One or two, depending on the size and strength," Sarah replied. "The sea monster is one, because that's evil nature's strongest spawn. But the Hubats, we can have as many as twenty, maybe thirty."

Perry, once again, felt ignorant and incompetent. These were things he was supposed to know.

"Correct," James said. "The people at the warehouse don't know it yet, but a pack of Hubats is headed their way."

"And so what?" Sarah said, unfazed. "Elite Mews have the warehouse surrounded. Your Father and Mother are there." She said it as though James's parents being there was supposed to reduce the threat to nil. "And if that's not enough, we have over one hundred Mews there. This is not a problem, James."

James's face remained dark.

Sarah saw this and said, "Except there's something else?"

Perry heard it first: super hearing and all. A disturbing outcry, somewhere between squawks of sea gulls and caws of crows, came from the Far East. Perry looked up and saw a massive black storm approach. As it got nearer, Perry's blood ran cold. The black storm that stretched from one end under the dark clouds all the way to the other was a host of bat-like creatures. They had wide bony wings. Their bodies were like that of a human being, although their legs were fused to form an arc, like the tail of a bird.

These creatures were larger than normal birds but a tad smaller than the aerial form of a Mew.

James pointed in the direction of the horde. "See for yourself," he said as Sarah followed his gaze and saw the swarm.

Sarah reeled and fell on her butt, trembling. "Hubats..." she muttered. "That's not possible."

James crawled to her and pulled her to her knees. "It's possible and it's happening," he said. "We need to move now."

"Are you crazy?" Sarah glared at James. "They'll tear us to pieces when they see us."

"Their eyes are set on something else," James said.

"The warehouse," Sarah gasped. "Our parents—"

"Can handle themselves," James replied. "We have to go now, otherwise, we'll miss the train." James helped her to her feet.

Perry took all this in, never once taking his eyes away from the Hubats. The flock had now formed a blanket over them, flapping towards the warehouse, squawking and cawing aloud. There must have been hundreds of them, if not thousands.

"Perry?" James asked. He and Sarah were already on the road.

Perry shot off his knees and followed them. They ran for a while before the dark blanket moved on. The warehouse was still a distance away, but with the sounds the Hubats were making, the Mews would have already been alerted. Perry found himself worrying about his parents. He still didn't understand what all this meant, and it frustrated him. James said Perry was the cause, the same way Perry was responsible for reawakening the sea monster. If the Mews found out about the Hubats, which they were about to, there was no way they would let him live.

They got to the train station without incidence. They bought three tickets and waited for the train on the platform. There were three normal-looking people also waiting for the train, so Perry felt safe.

The train pulled up a few minutes later. The three boarded the train and found an empty car. The train was underway in seconds. On the train coming to Brooklyn, Sarah had sat close to Perry; now, James sat in between Perry and Sarah. Perry thought about apologizing to Sarah, but there were more important things to discuss with James. Things like what next, now that evil nature was strong. If it takes a whole pack or clan of Mews to defeat twenty Hubats, how many would it take to defeat a thousand?

"James," Sarah said, "do you think we lost the Red Tails?"

James shrugged.

"Don't you think it's odd, though," she pressed, furrowing her brow. She was deep in thought. "That they should leave the meeting just before the Hubats showed up?"

"They were pursuing us, Sarah," James said.

"Yeah, but they never really followed us after we left the warehouse, did they? I mean, they should have pursued us *until* we met the Hubats. Then, they could have run or stood and fought. But we lost them in the skies."

"You think they have something to do with the Hubat attack? Like treachery?" James had an incredulous look in his eyes.

Sarah bobbed her head. "It's worth considering."

"What if it's a trap?" Perry asked. "What if they're out there waiting to attack us?"

There was a silence.

Sarah scowled at him and slumped against the metal seat. James remained silent. He seemed relieved to not have to talk about the incidence with the Hubats. Perry knew that back at the warehouse the Fortins would be at the forefront of the battle, which predisposed them to harm more than others.

Perry took one brief look at James. James had a tight grimace on his face. He was holding back apprehension. It was possible that his parents wouldn't come back to the house today. It was possible that they would die in battle. *To lose one's whole family in a day*, Perry thought, *that must leave a scar.*

Perry laid a hand on the boy's shoulder.

James turned and looked at him. His eyes were clouded by tears.

"They're going to be fine," Perry said, smiling.

James swallowed. A single teardrop fell from his eye. "How do you know?"

"If what I saw on the platform between our parents is real, then my parents will fight alongside your parents. They'll make it together."

James was about to reply when he was cut short by a sudden rattle. The door before them that led between cars opened abruptly and five men trooped into the car. Perry recognized two of them as fast as Sarah did.

Perry jerked out of the bench and retreated towards the other end of the car. James followed him, but Sarah made a stand in the path of the men.

The men stopped, not sure whether to pass by Sarah.

Don and Chase pushed through the three men until they were before Sarah.

Don, the eldest of the three siblings, smiled and pushed his arms apart in a welcoming gesture. "Thank you, Sister," he said in a loud voice, "for bringing the eagle to us. You have done your part. Let us do ours. Stand aside."

Perry's gaze slowly fell from Don's muscular face and fierce eyes to Sarah. She chanced a glance at him and looked back at her brother.

"What are you doing?" she muttered to Don. Sarah seemed mad. "This was not the plan."

"Ah," Chase replied. "But you see, we changed the plan." Chase looked up at Perry. His face tightened with anger. "We can't wait any longer. We want him now." Chase, Sarah's more handsome and less affable brother, grabbed Sarah and threw her to one of the other men to hold down. Sarah screamed and kicked, but they were efforts in futility, the big burly man having her tightly clamped down. Sarah's brothers and the remaining men advanced on Perry and James.

Perry was shocked. His eyes locked with Sarah's in a stinging grip of betrayal. He didn't yet realize he was frozen until James pulled him towards the door. Everything seemed to slow down. Sarah's thrashing. The men's advance. James's voice was like a hollow disturbance in his ears telling him they had to leave now. They pushed through the door onto the gangway connection where they climbed up to the roof of the train. It all happened so fast. The next Perry knew, he and James were wobbling on the roof of the trembling train, which was hurtling towards Manhattan in the dark at about one hundred and twenty miles per hour.

"We have to fly!" James yelled into Perry's ear. They were both bent a little so that their hands were ready to grab the roof of the train should the train shake too terribly.

"It's a trap," Perry replied. "The Red Tails are waiting for us beyond those clouds. I can't believe she would betray me."

"She betrayed us both, Perry," James replied.

Don and Chase climbed onto the roof of the train. Chase, still enraged, charged at them.

James jumped in front of Perry and charged back. "Take off, Perry," James yelled, "it is no longer safe here."

James collided with Chase, sending him off balance. Before he fell to the roof of the car, Chase swatted James to the side. James spiraled off the edge of the roof and was yanked backwards and out of sight by an invisible force. The last Perry heard of his friend was a holler that immediately gave way to silence.

Chase struggled to his feet. Perry turned away, ran to the edge, and jumped. He felt a strong wind push him backwards. His eagle form came forth with a blinding flash of light. Perry spread his wings and rose away from the train tracks. He hovered for a while, his first thought to go see if James was still alive. But then, he heard wings.

The flaps were soft, and the air a silent whoosh around the wings. They were deliberately trying to mask their flight. He orbited his position once, scanning his surroundings and the dark clouds above him. He saw nothing, yet he heard them approach. His eye sight wasn't good in the night. However, his hearing didn't diminish with the setting of the sun. He could *hear* the Red Tails flying towards him. Judging by their speed and distance, they would be upon him in a minute.

Perry's heart picked up pace.

He steered away from the train tracks and soared into a residential neighborhood. He stretched his wings, the winds carrying him higher and higher. *Maybe if I fly high enough,* he thought, *they won't be able to catch me.* He was wrong.

The Red Tails already had the advantage of height. So, before he could rise beyond their range, they struck. Like bullets, they fell upon him, their claws snatching feathers, snatching flesh. A searing pain tore through his brain. Perry tried to fight back. Tried to spin and claw. But, the Red Tails that attacked him were like vicious ghosts in the night. He never saw them coming. He never saw them going. The only thing he knew of their attack was the sharp pain somewhere on his body and the trickle of blood that followed. The pain became so unbearable that Perry lost focus on trying to stay afloat. He began to plummet like a falling star.

As he fell through the sky, he took note of an area to the north that had a large building in it—an area that was shrouded in darkness. It was a three-story house with a wiry frame shaped like a crooked needle. He strangely felt drawn to the house, the same way he felt drawn to the sea monster in his dreams.

Nothing good can come out of hiding in the house, Perry decided. Still, if he didn't seek refuge in that house, for at least a minute, the Red Tails would kill him. So, Perry summoned the last of his strength. He had reeled in his wings to protect them from the Red Tails attack. That way, they didn't hurt too much. Now, he spread them out, flexing and causing the flow of wind around his form to change. The sudden effect began to angle him towards the open window on the third floor. *Pilots called it controlled descent,* Perry remarked to himself with satisfaction. He wasn't a total dullard after all.

The wind did as he desired, carrying him in the direction of the house's open third floor window.

In his periphery, he saw five birds clear the dark clouds and be revealed by whatever light there was. They hung in the sky, flapping to remain afloat but not venturing further than the belly of the clouds. They did not dive for the kill, even though they had the upper hand. Perry flew through the window and flapped to control his speedy ingress. He failed, crashing into the dusty wooden floor. He began to lose consciousness immediately.

Before he blacked out, he heard someone approach. He had fallen into a small stuffy bedroom. The door to the bedroom was closed. But out there, someone knew he was in the house. They knew and were headed towards him. The person approached him slow and deliberate. Taunting Perry—knowing he could never escape. Perry knew he had left the frying pan. He was now in the fire.

15

PERRY JOHNSON AND THE ONE-EYED WITCH

P erry knew when she entered the bedroom, an old scraggly woman.

He knew when she closed the windows. He knew when she carried him down a staircase for about ten minutes to a dank underground cave. He knew when she threw his eagle form into a dungeon and locked the door. He wasn't fully conscious. All he had were glimpses. However, these glimpses were enough to cause him to feel dread when he stirred on the musty floor sometime later.

His first reaction was to push away from the iron bars of his prison to the opposite wall, dragging wet black sand with his clothes. Beyond the gates, there was a wide room with a ceiling that was beyond Perry's view. In the center of the room, there was a cauldron on a fire and a black-clad woman, who used a crooked stick to stir the content of the black pot.

"Yes, yes, yes," the woman muttered to herself, giggling sinisterly. She stirred the large pot with her body, sort of dancing around the fire. "The eagle has come to stay..." The woman turned her head to Perry's right.

"Yes, yes, yes," said a choked-up voice with a high pitch. "An eagle we shall slay." Then, they both let out a shrill laughter.

Perry swallowed, pulling his knees to his chest.

To the left was a winding stairway without a rail guard that rose into the air. Perry crawled towards the door following the stairs until it terminated in a door in the wall. Perry was an eagle and therefore wasn't afraid of heights. But seeing the crooked steps rise like a spine three floors into the air made him feel queasy. Then, he looked at the woman. She was old and barely able to stand. Her black drabs were tattered. She turned and Perry saw that she was missing an eye. Her nose was pointy and crooked. Her hands were bony and gnarled. Her body was thin and twisted. Perry wondered how she had survived the descent down such a treacherous set of steps.

The ceiling was a short distance above the door. It was made of an obsidian rock, as though the gigantic cave had been carved out of the ground. They were no doubt beneath ground level. Opposite the one-eyed woman was a long table. On this table were various objects, long and short knives with embedded rubies in them, and scattered groceries. To the right there was a sofa overstuffed with pillows, and on the pillows lay a horrid inhuman creature. He looked like a stout hunchback that couldn't have been more than four feet tall. It was this creature that had the choked, high-pitched voice, and he was staring at Perry with black, clouded eyes.

"Eagle," the creature quipped, excited. It had stalks for hands. Nonetheless, it jabbed these stalks in excitement. "Eagle. The eagle is finally awake!"

"What?" The woman jerked to the creature first, as if it had disturbed a trance of hers. Then, she turned to face Perry.

Perry stiffened under the woman's fierce gaze.

The woman took three quick steps towards the prison. Perry pushed back until he slammed into the rough wall behind him.

The woman crouched at the gate and examined him with a sneer. "Tell me, boy," she said in a shrill voice, "do you feel any pain, any weakness?"

Perry shook his head, utterly speechless. He wasn't feeling any pain, which was strange since he had blacked out, bleeding on the wooden floor of the bedroom. But why was she asking? Had she healed him? If so, how and why? She certainly did not look like a good person. And what was that creature on the couch looking at him?

The old woman returned to the pot and her stirring.

"Why...why do you have me locked up...locked up in a prison... ma'am?" Perry asked, stuttering over his words.

The woman looked over her shoulder at Perry. "So you won't escape. What do you think, boy?"

"But what do you need me for?"

The woman stayed her hands and fully turned to meet his gaze. "You know little for an eagle Mew, you know that?"

Perry shrugged. "There's not much to learn when every Mew in the country is out to get you."

The woman and the creature both laughed out loud.

"I like this one, Buba," the woman said to the creature.

"Me, too," Buba replied.

Then the woman's face turned serious. She approached the prison again, this time taking deliberate steps as she spoke. "Have you not heard tales of a certain house on a certain street in Brooklyn?" She said it as if it were a nursery rhyme, one that every Mew should have learned. One that his parents hadn't seen fit to tell him. Again. Only this time, it may cost him his life.

"My parents never told me about this house, ma'am," Perry said. He hoped if he convinced the woman that he didn't mean to crash into her house, she would let him go. He had a feeling that that stirring in the pot was in preparation for something bigger. "I've only been an eagle for a few days, and since then I've been on the run for my life. I don't know much about Mews. I was chased by red-tailed kites to this place. They would have killed me had I not entered your house."

The woman looked at him, her one eye filling with mock compassion. Then she cocked her head upwards, put her hands on her belly, and let out a thunderous laugh. "Don't be silly, boy! It's not something your parents tell you. It's something your clan chief tells you."

Perry felt his eyebrow rise as he remembered his clan chief referencing a certain house on a certain street in Brooklyn just after the Fall Ritual. Perry had been too taken up by his family's strange behavior that he hadn't heard what the chief had said about the house. Only that he was to avoid it at all cost. His heart sank as his shoulders dropped.

The woman turned to Buba. "He remembers, Buba." She faced him, drawing nearer with each word. "If you had been, say, a kite or a falcon, you would not even wake up alive." Her voice was low and had daggers in them. Daggers that cut at Perry's heart. "But since you are an eagle, the very eagle that was forespoken to turn the tides for nature's misunderstood aspect, we kept you alive."

"By misunderstood aspect could you be referring to evil nature?" Perry asked even though he already knew the answer to that question.

The woman laughed again. "Is that what you call her nowadays? Evil nature?" And just like that, anger descended on the old woman's face. Every shred of humor vanished in an instant. "It doesn't matter anymore. Because your sacrifice tonight will release her in her full glory and every Mew who would stand against her will feel the full power of her wrath."

Perry's heartbeat spiked several folds. "My sacrifice?"

The woman scoffed. "Yes, Eagle. Your sacrifice. You see those markings over there on the wall?"

Perry followed the woman's finger to the wall behind Buba. There was a circular diagram with strange markings etched into the wall. Perry didn't understand them, neither could he describe them.

"That diagram appears rarely. It's a portal, and you are the key."

"A portal to where?"

"A portal to release evil nature, stupid boy," Buba replied and gave a throaty laughter.

"Once I spill your blood and guts into this cauldron," the woman said, "one sprinkle of the soup will open the portal. Then chaos will reign supreme!" She cackled and continued stirring. "It's almost ready, Eagle. Just a few more minutes."

Perry grabbed the bars of the iron and shook it hard. "You will never succeed, Witch!" Perry yelled. "The Mews will come for me. They will find you and destroy you."

"What Mew?" the one-eyed witch replied, stopping for a moment. "What Mew, Perry Johnson?"

Perry's heart caught in his chest. He backed away from the iron bars.

"Yes," the witch whispered. "How do you suppose I know your name? How do you suppose you were chased to this particular location? Of all the places for the train trap to be sprung, why near here? Yes, I know about the train trap. There are Mews who see the coming disaster to the Mewranters and have chosen life instead of death. Too bad you don't get the same offer."

"The Red Tails, the Crofts, Sarah?"

"Don't be silly, kid," the witch replied. "Treachery amongst the Mews runs deeper. Deeper than anyone knows. Deeper than you can fathom. You, boy, will be the end of the Mews."

"If I die," Perry said, "then the sea monster dies."

"Not if you die in this stew, it doesn't." The witch walked over to the table, picked some carrots, tomatoes, and a palm length object that looked like a wine opener and dumped all of them into the seething cauldron. She continued to stir.

"The sea monster is Mother Nature's strongest creation," Buba said, "but now that her power has risen, now that she is about to be released, there will be more horrors to come."

"Tell me, Buba," Perry said, suspecting that Buba was a talker, "can the sea monster be destroyed?"

"Of course it can be destroyed," Buba replied. "Nothing is indestructible. Cut out its eyes—"

"Buba!" The witch glared at Buba. "Shut up!"

Buba retreated further into the pillows. "Yes, Mother," he said in a submissive tone.

"There's no escape for you, Perry," the witch said. "The sea monster will see all Mews in America dead, before it sets its sight on Africa. And that paltry task force currently searching for the monster is headed for their doom. The sea monster is right under their noses and they do not yet realize it." She glanced at the table and groaned. "Buba, watch our prisoner. I left the gut cutter in the attic."

Buba chuckled excitedly as the witch climbed the steps. "With pleasure, Mother," he said.

Perry crawled to the iron bars again and watched the witch ascend, taking strenuous steps. Buba jabbed his stalks together, giggling. Once the woman disappeared behind the door, Perry settled down on the ground. The moment the witch returned, his throat would be slit. That would be the end of it. *Maybe it's good,* Perry thought to himself. At least then he wouldn't have to worry about the sea monster.

After one long minute, the door opened again. Perry refused to look up. He didn't want to see what the gut cutter looked like earlier than necessary.

"Perr, are you there?" Someone whispered. It didn't sound like the one-eyed witch.

Perry scrambled to his feet and looked up. His heart jumped at what he saw. On the small landing high up stood James. And Sarah. They were looking down in search of him.

"I'm down here!" Perry yelled, waving his hands through the bars of iron to catch their attention. It worked.

"Shush, quiet, Perry," James whispered. "The witch won't be gone much longer. We're coming down to get you."

Buba began to jabber, nervous.

James leaped off the landing, followed by Sarah. They transformed seconds off the ledge and transformed back close to the ground, landing with a crouch. Sarah ran to the prison gate, ignoring Buba's noisome threats. Her face was moist with tears, her eyes looking pleadingly into Perry's.

"What's she doing here, James?" Perry asked, wary of Sarah.

James came to the gates with a bunch of keys. He fiddled with it, looking for the right one. "It was a trick," James said. "They were trying to divide us. They had me convinced, until Sarah came back to help me. She was the one who found out you were being held here."

The moment James pulled open the door Sarah was in Perry's arms. They remained locked in an embrace for a while.

"Perr," she whispered, "I'm so sorry. I'm sorry about what my brothers did to you."

Perry's heart melted. Tears began to fill his eyes. "I thought you betrayed us."

"I would never!" Sarah replied vehemently, breaking their embrace with a straight look on her face.

"No, no, no," Buba cried, agitated, cutting through their moment. "You cannot escape. You are the sacrifice."

Perry led Sarah out of the prison. He left her standing beside James and walked over to the cauldron.

"Oh yeah?" Perry said, pulling out the stirring stick. It was hot to touch. "Well hear this. The sacrifice is off. Evil nature will remain locked in the portal forever." Perry struck the cauldron once with the stick and tipped it over, spilling thick greenish goo on the floor. A swish of black smoke uncurled from the miasma, coiling its way up through the air. At five yards above their heads, it disintegrated in a puff of black mist and vanished. Immediately, a foul odor settled upon them. They all turned their heads away from the smell, but whatever power the one-eyed witch had concocted in the cauldron was gone.

A shrill shriek rent the air.

Perry's head jerked up to the landing to see the witch standing on the ledge glaring down at the trio.

James and Sarah formed around him.

"Do you have your transothe?" James whispered, his eyes never leaving the one-eyed witch.

"Yes," Perry replied, "but she's mine. Once I attack her, you go on ahead. Lead us out of here. I'll follow behind."

"If you don't follow, we're coming back," Sarah said with an edge in her voice.

Perry smiled. He really did miss her. He lurched towards the stairs and left the ground with a hard push. He transformed into a massive golden eagle and shot towards the witch. The witch transformed into a horrid Hubat. That was saying something since Hubats were naturally horrid looking. However, the blinding flash that attended his transformation caught her off guard and disoriented her. Perry grabbed the creature's chest with his talons and whipped her around, bashing her with his massive wings, as a white owl and a black falcon shot past them. His wings were bigger than he remembered, each now about three yards away from his chest. He knew he should be getting worried at his growing size.

Perry flung the Hubat towards the ground and shot up after his friends. Through the door, they had to ascend another flight of stairs, though this one was encased within a narrow stairwell. This slowed their progress since their wings were too big to fit well. By the time they got to a corridor, the Hubat was hot on their tail. It was now bigger, with huger fangs coming out of its mouth. Something told Perry its transformation wasn't yet complete.

They came into a wide lobby. There was an open window beside the door. James sped for it and they followed. Perry could smell the fresh air of freedom, before a shriek from the Hubat behind them caused the windows to slam shut. James crashed into the glass without denting it. Instead of slamming into James, Sarah broke her speed and spun, ascending the air. Perry followed her with James bringing up the rear. They rose to the second floor and soared into another corridor. As they neared open windows, the Hubat would shriek and the windows would slam shut. With each window slamming shut, the creature was closing in.

Then a thought struck Perry's mind.

"*Attic,*" he said to James, taking the lead in the race.

"*Did you just speak to me, Perry?*" James asked.

"*Oh my god,*" Sarah said in awe. They flew into a stairwell and flapped, upwards.

"*Uh, guys, whatever you think the witch did to me, she didn't. She didn't have enough time before you guys came. So, I can still speak quite well.*"

"*It's not that, Perr,*" Sarah said. "*You do realize we are in our aerial forms. We shouldn't be able to communicate except if we are clan or family...*"

"*Or we've developed a primal link with each other,*" James concluded. "*We are now a team, Perry. And to Mews, team has a whole new definition.*"

"*Can we talk about this when the sea monster is dead?*" Perry said, fleeing into the attic. To his relief, the window was open. It was made of wood, unlike the other windows. But the window didn't stay open. The shriek came, light and distant (Hubats found it more difficult to fly upstairs), however, it had the same effect. The windows slammed shut.

The closed windows didn't deter him. His parents were probably part of the task force, which was headed for doom. He had to get out of here at all cost and warn them. Perry put more power to his wings and drove headlong into the wood. It broke apart on impact, letting Perry into the open air. Perry extended his wings full length. The wind rushed around him, sucking him upwards, welcoming him—king of the winds—back. Perry relished the rush of the wind through his plumage. His heart flushed with respite. He was free. And he knew how to kill the sea monster.

16
THE TASK FORCE

Perry's eagle joined up with Sarah's owl and James's falcon after a while. They flew, silent, for miles in the direction of Manhattan. Day had dawned. They soared between bright white clouds, veering and bending with the twisting train track below, which was their only guide. The tracks traversed an area where shrubs dotted the landscape. They descended and flew close to the ground. When they got to the place where the train tracks turned west and headed into the city, James led them on northwards until an abandoned building rose over the horizon.

They circled the fenceless structure first, Perry especially searching far and wide for incoming threats. The sun was already rising upwards and the sky had become cloudless and clear. The building beneath them had catwalks attached to it and nylon sheets draping its walls and swaying in the soft wind that came in from the south. Observing no threats, James spiraled to the ground and the others followed suit. They transformed smoothly and stood facing the building.

"Why have you brought us here?" Perry asked James.

"There's something you need to know," Sarah answered.

"Also, there's someone you need to meet," James said.

"Okay, let's go," Perry said and started towards the entrance, which was a vaulted archway. He stopped and turned. Sarah and James hadn't moved. "Aren't you coming?"

"He wants to meet with you alone," James replied. "Don't worry. He's a family friend."

Perry looked at the building once more. It looked like a church building with its high vaulted windows and archways. There wasn't another structure for miles, except the train tracks. There wasn't a fence or a demarcation to separate it from the wild shrubs that formed the whole area. There was absolutely no reason why the building should exist where it did.

Perry was suspicious. This was most likely a trap. *Treachery amongst the Mews runs deeper. Deeper than anyone knows,* the one-eyed witch had said. Perry could not trust anyone. But Sarah and James didn't know of this treachery. If this were a trap, they wouldn't know. Perry turned around and walked back to them. If they took off now, before the trap was sprung, they could evade capture.

Perry stood in front of the two, leaned his head forward into them, and spoke in a low but firm voice. "Look, I don't have time for this," he began, letting too much anger into his voice than he had intended. "The task force of which my parents and James's parents are a part of is currently headed for doom"—Sarah's expression changed—"and if we don't leave now to warn them, they might die."

Sarah looked at James. "We need to warn them."

James shook his head. "No. He has to meet him. He has to know. This is more important."

"You don't understand, James," Perry said.

"I understand real well," James replied, his voice slightly shaky with apprehension. "My parents are on that task force, too. If what you say is true, then their lives are in danger."

Perry observed the boy. His face had lost color, his shoulders sagged, and his choppy hair was dusty.

"There's more," Perry said, reducing his voice to a whisper. "The witch that had me imprisoned, she said that there were Mews who had sided with evil nature. Mews that thought there was a coming apocalypse, and so joined forces with evil nature. In her own words: *Treachery amongst the Mews runs deep. Deeper than anyone knows.*"

"I suspected as much," a voice boomed behind him.

Perry jerked around. Standing akimbo in the vaulted doorway was Mr. Monte, regal in his black outfit. He had a smug look on his face. "This is why I need to speak to you. Come." Mr. Monte turned and retreated into the building.

Perry took one last look at his friends. They motioned for him to follow. Perry turned and followed into the building. The archway he went through was at the end of the building and led into a large hollow hall that spanned the length of the building. It was a church, or at least would have been a church had the project been completed. There were catwalks and building materials scattered around in the hall. Ahead, the altar seemed to have been completed. Mr. Monte headed in that direction, crisscrossing the litter in the room. Perry followed him.

"You know," Mr. Monte said, "you and I are clan." He paused for a response, but Perry remained quiet and followed.

"Your clan chief is my father, and that makes me a member of the clan. I had my Fall Ritual years ago and was inducted into the clan. But now, I'm a partial member because I owe allegiance to the Central Council, which is not the most popular of positions a Mew can have." A certain gloom came over Mr. Monte. This lengthened their progress through the metal wreck towards the cleared altar. Perry's eyes rose to the high windows to his right. Rays of light poured into the massive hall, chasing away darkness from every nook and cranny of the room. In the rays, dust particles danced, bobbed, and moved; oblivious to the two figures that picked their way to the altar. The altar was a large two feet podium that was fused to this end of the building.

Mr. Monte arrived at the altar. He sat and motioned for Perry to sit beside him. Mr. Monte's head was bowed as though he were recalling some sadness in his past. Perry observed the sour smile on his face.

"Sir," Perry said, "why have you called me here?"

Mr. Monte seemed to snap out of his reverie. The air of sadness had vanished, replaced by a shroud of secrecy. Mr. Monte's eyes narrowed, his voice becoming a whisper. "These lands are uninhabited," he began, casting furtive glances through the windows that paneled the sides of the hall. "So, it's safe to talk. Perry, as you already know, treachery runs deep amongst our type. There are Mews who have aligned themselves with evil nature. I've always suspected this, but because I didn't have any hard evidence, I couldn't be sure. But with what happened at the general clan meeting, I became sure." Mr. Monte's eyebrow went up when he saw the look on Perry's face. "You haven't heard about the clan meeting?"

Perry shook his head. How could he? He was locked up in a dungeon.

"We were attacked," Mr. Monte said. "Now, you might not understand why that's such a big deal, but this is the first time it's happened. The location of the general clan meeting is only known to the clan chiefs of all the clans participating. These chiefs are required to bring their members to the meeting. No creature of evil could have known where we were had it not been told to them by one of us. A clan chief to be precise."

Mr. Monte paused and sucked in a lungful of breath. Light glinted off his eyes. "We have never seen Hubats in that number before. Mews were wasted in the tens. We defeated the Hubats, but at great cost."

"So why tell me all this?" Perry asked, confused. "If you know there are traitors amongst us, report it to the Central Council."

Mr. Monte searched Perry's eyes before he replied. "Because there are traitors on the Council itself."

That revelation hit Perry, broadside.

"There are fourteen members on the council," Mr. Monte continued. "At least one of them is a traitor."

There was a silence. Even in Perry's mind, there was a silence.

Why would a Mew ruler ever align himself with his greatest enemy? As the question came up in Perry's mind an answer followed. *Because he believes there is no way Mews can survive evil nature's rise to power.*

"Perry, listen and listen well," Mr. Monte said. "I'm not going to lie to you. Things don't look good for you. People know that the only reason evil nature is getting stronger is that the sea monster is getting stronger, which is because you are still alive. With the massacre at the warehouse, people will be coming for your life. And I don't blame them."

Mr. Monte eyed Perry before continuing. "Not much is known about your kind. People are afraid of what they do not know. But there is something I know about eagles. They are a scepter of justice. It's not just about the powers you have, Perry. It's about what the powers are for. By right, you are one third the ruler of the Mews and head of the Central Council. You're a threat to the powers that be. This is why I've called you here."

"Why," Perry blurted, his voice choked. He swallowed hard, a coldness all over him.

"So you can know what you're up against," Mr. Monte answered. "Whether you like it or not, Perry, trouble has come to you. You can either do something about the traitors in our midst or not. But this is me, bringing the ruler of the Mews a report on the state of our people."

"I have to go," Perry replied, jumped on his feet, and ran away from the altar.

"Perry!" Mr. Monte called.

"I have to go," Perry said again. He crossed the archway.

Sarah and James were sitting on the edge of the terrace. When they saw Perry pass, they jerked up to their feet and raced to meet him. Perry kept walking, letting his eagle rise.

"What did he say?" Sarah asked. She and James were looking in his direction as they matched his hurried pace.

"There are traitors in the Central Council," Perry replied. As for the rest, Perry decided Mr. Monte was crazy.

Sarah and James, especially James, looked stunned.

After a tensed silence, Perry said, "Let's fly."

They nodded in acquiescence. "Where to?" James asked.

"To warn our parents," Perry replied, breaking into a run. His eagle was ready to come forth.

"You don't know where they are," James said, he and Sarah running beside him.

Perry smiled. "Oh, I know." He leaped into the air, and with a satisfying release, his body transformed into a huge golden eagle. Beside him, he saw Sarah's owl and James's falcon burst forth with the same fluidity. It was as if functioning as a Mew was easier around the two. They rose into the air at bullet speed.

The wind was on their side.

Perry looked over his shoulder. The building would, no doubt, now be a distant speck in the shrubby landscape to James and Sarah, but not to Perry. He clearly saw the expression on Mr. Monte's face; it was that of sorrow. Perry thought that the expression complemented his black outfit. At least now, he was really mourning.

They followed the train tracks into Manhattan, but as soon as they got to the city, Perry yielded himself to the constant pull to the sea he felt in his heart. If the sea monster had set a trap for the task force, then wherever the monster was, there would be the task force.

At first, it was difficult to follow the pull. They sort of drifted through the sky, flying all over Manhattan with no particular direction to go in. But then, Perry caught a strong "signal" that led them to a private dock on the Hudson River. The dock was deserted. There was no ship at berth. They fell to the ground, transforming back before touching the wooden dock. Two minutes later, they picked themselves from the wet floor. It was easier transforming fluidly back to human form earlier on at the abandoned church. Maybe, the difficulty had something to do with the fear that ran through their little bodies.

A strange mist covered the river, spilling over the dock, despite the sun. Somewhere out there in the river, he could feel the sea monster wriggling along, waiting to strike. Perry had never felt the pull so strong before. He swayed.

Sarah held him. "Are you all right?" she asked.

Perry steadied himself and sighed. "Yeah. Let's split up. Sarah, you check the offices. James, you check the entrance to the dock while I check the dock itself."

They didn't like it, but they agreed anyway and separated.

Perry started walking along the dock keeping a safe distance from the water even before his eyes adjusted to the mist. *I'm not here to fight the monster,* he thought to himself. He was here to warn the task force of the trap they were currently walking into.

In the distance, he saw a pack of about eight people. At first, he thought they were workers. But then, he recognized Richard's voice. Before he could shout to get their attention, he felt a strong force like a magnet yank him towards the water. Perry stumbled backwards, fighting the pull. He felt like he was being sucked into a cyclone, but there was no such stirring; there were no strings attached to him. He looked over his shoulder at the waters. He saw a blurry green creature move beneath the surface.

Perry's heart jumped. And then he followed suit, his eagle coming forth with a blinding flash. He shot upwards just as the creature broke through the wood of the dock where he had been standing not too long ago. There was a great sound like a snarl. Splinters flew in every direction. When Perry looked back, the sea monster was gone. What remained was a hole in the dock.

17
ATTACKED AGAIN

Perry kept on rising. He didn't feel safe anywhere close to that dock. He would have flown away if it weren't for Sarah and James, who were still around and in danger. His heart raced. He found an antenna pole and landed on it. He watched as Mews gathered around the hole. Six, including Richard, Perry's father, and James's father, jumped into the water after the sea monster.

Sarah and James ran into view, surprising Perry's and James's mothers.

"What are you kids doing here?!" Mrs. Fortin bellowed. "James, you should know better!"

James shuddered but Sarah was unfazed.

Joanna scanned the duo with a cross-examining eye, and then said, "I think the more important question is, where is Perry?"

"He was right here," James explained. Perry could not tell if his shivering was because of their brush with the sea monster or his mother's condescending presence.

"Well then, he couldn't have gone far, could he?" Joanna said, almost lazily, as if his probable presence here was okay. Both women scanned the dock, low and high, until their eyes fell on him high up the pole. Perry shot out his wings and sprung from the pole, noting the look of astonishment on Mrs. Fortin's face. Most people had heard of an eagle Mew; only a few had actually seen one up close. Perry transformed back to his human form several feet away from the group, falling flat on his face.

Sarah and James were already at his side. They helped him to his feet, and together the trio approached the two women. Mother's hair was pulled back in a ponytail while James's mother's hair flowed down to her shoulders. James's mother was a little bit taller than his. They both wore tight blue pants and jackets. Perry's mother's jacket was white while James's mother's was green.

Perry stepped closer to his mother. Her stormy grey eyes looked into his. He couldn't tell whether she was furious with him or not.

Perry cleared his throat. Looking between his mother and James's mother, Daphne, he said, "We came to warn you of the sea monster. You were walking into a trap. We couldn't sit back at home doing nothing while you were walking into your doom."

Joanna closed her eyes momentarily. She crouched before him, pulled him close with both hands, and hugged him. He could feel her heart beating fast. She was scared.

"You did a brave thing, Perr," Joanna said. "But you could have gotten James or Sarah or yourself hurt."

"We were willing to take the risk," James blurted, defiance in his voice.

"James!" Daphne rebuked the boy.

"What?" James replied. Mother and son exchanged looks.

Joanna smiled at him and ruffled his hair. "You look tired," she said. "Have you been awake all night?"

Perry nodded. He began to feel tired.

"Perry, your father and I love you very much," she said. "We don't know what we would do should anything happen to you." She paused. There was bitterness in her voice. Perry couldn't tell why. He looked over his shoulder at Sarah and James. They shrugged. Perry wondered what decision had been made at the general clan meeting.

"Perry."

Perry gazed back at his mother.

"Mrs. Fortin, here, will take you and your friends home. Stay there until your father or I return. It's not safe for you to be away from Jake or any of us for now. Is that understood?"

Perry nodded.

Joanna stood and closed the distance between herself and Mrs. Fortin. They spoke in hushed tones, but Perry heard every word.

"They've been in the water too long," Joanna said.

"I know," Daphne replied with a worried look.

"Take them to their houses and return," Joanna said. "I'll go in after them."

"Be safe." Daphne turned and walked away. "Come," she called to them without looking back.

Perry glanced at his mother. She nodded for him to go.

Perry, Sarah, and James followed Daphne to a black SUV parked in the deserted parking lot. James sat with his mother in front while Perry and Sarah packed into the spacious back. They drove in silence until they arrived at Sarah's house.

Sarah hugged Perry. "I'm glad you're safe," she whispered into his ears. She touched James's shoulder. "Bye, James."

"Bye," James replied, lightly tapping her fingers on his shoulder.

"Thanks for the ride, Mrs. Fortin," Sarah said, looking into the rear-view mirror.

"Take care of yourself, young lady," Mrs. Fortin replied.

Sarah smiled at Perry again before coming down. She shut the door and trudged up the driveway to their house. Mrs. Fortin drove off.

When they got to the front of Perry's family's apartment building, James came down to say goodbye. He put forward his hands, but Perry disregarded the hand and hugged him. "Thanks for everything," he said in a low tone and pulled away.

"It's not over," James said. "I wish we could have done more, you know."

Perry nodded, thoughtful for a while. He recalled Mr. Monte's words. He had not yet told his friends about his conversation with Mr. Monte. "Something tells me before the week is over, we'll do more.

"When I saw the sea monster back at the dock today, I panicked. I ran away. But I know I'm going to have to face the monster before this can end." Perry thought for a moment, then said, "I hope you're not getting into trouble with your parents because of me."

James scowled. "My parents? Seriously?"

"I heard that," Mrs. Fortin said at the steering wheels. "Aren't you forgetting something?"

James's eyebrows arched in realization. "Perry, the transothe. My Mother wants to return it."

Perry retrieved the brown material from his pocket and handed it over to James.

"Bye, Perry." James got back into the vehicle.

Perry waved as the vehicle pulled back into the traffic and drove off. Perry was about to head up when he caught the steady gaze of a man. He was tall and muscular and stood across the street from him, staring directly at Perry, his eyes full of murderous intent. Perry looked away as if he didn't think it was unusual for people to stare. He turned to the doorway of the apartment and ran up the stairs.

By the time he got to the door of their apartment, every bone and joint in his body creaked with pain. His eyes were sodden with sleep. He wanted to knock on the door, but then thought about it and tried opening it first. To his surprise, the door opened. He entered the apartment and shut the door quietly. As he walked by, he glanced into the living room. Jake was still asleep on the couch. Perry's eyes immediately flew across the room to the clock. It was already eight.

Perry chuckled and dragged his body to his room. He took a quick hot shower, putting on new clothes the moment he was out and dried. He fell on his bed, fatigued beyond measure. So fatigued that when he slept seconds later, he did not dream.

◆　◆　◆

The bang on the boarded-up window jerked him out of his sleep. His eyes stung with drowsiness. Perry glanced around the semi-darkness, wondering where and *when* he was. There were three more bangs in quick succession. The boards fell through with a crack, flooding the room with sunlight. Perry jumped out of bed and reared away from the open window. He remembered everything and knew that an open window was not a good thing.

The door opened. Jake ran inside holding Perry's bag in his hands.

"Perry," he said, panting, "you ready?"

Perry nodded and took the bag. He didn't know what he was ready for, but he was ready nonetheless.

"Do you have your transothe on you?" Jake ran to the window. He looked through. Three seconds later, his eyes widened and his mouth fell open.

Perry rummaged through the bag, pulled out his transothe, and tucked it into his pocket.

Jake grabbed Perry's hands and dragged him out of the room just as a huge bird shot through the opening. He locked the door and pulled Perry into the sitting room. They waited at the door into the house. Beyond the door, Perry could hear growls. It could have been a lion, or a tiger, or one of a number of wildland predators.

"What's happening?" Perry asked, his heart picking pace.

"We're under attack," Jake said, listening to the throaty growl. "They're waiting for us outside. They probably have the air surrounded. I'm going to transform into my terrestrial form and attack the beast outside. When I do that, I want you to fly through the roof. You're faster than any Mew bird alive. Get away from here and head to the cabin. We'll meet you there." Just then, Perry heard a loud bang coming from his room. Someone was trying to break his door.

Jake opened the door without warning. Immediately, an impossibly large—Mew large—beast leaped on Jake. He caught the beast by its neck, and together they rolled into the apartment. Jake began to transform. Perry spared not another second. He lurched out of the apartment and ran up the stairs, taking the steps three at a time. Below, he heard hurried footsteps following him. He counted three people.

Perry's phone rang. He rummaged through his bag, retrieved his phone, and answered the call, all the while bounding upwards.

"Perr?" It was Sarah.

"Yeah?"

She heaved a sigh of relief. "Thank God, you're alive! You need to get out of your house right now! The sea monster has struck again, and this time, more than twenty Mews were killed. They're coming for you."

"Who is?"

"Sarah!" A voice called to her in the background.

Sarah's voice dropped to a whisper. "I've got to go. Get out of there now and stay low." The line went dead.

The door to the roof was open. He ran onto the gravel surface, high-tailing it to the west end. He chanced a glance at the sky and his heart sank. High up in the clouds, there were Mew birds circling. Large, powerful looking raptors that started an attack dive the moment they saw him. Perry didn't count, but he knew there couldn't be less than fifteen. Fifteen highly trained Mews had come after a hatchling. He didn't know whether to be flattered or scared. Perry put his phone back into the bag and threw the bag into a corner. He got to the edge of the roof of the fifteen-story building and jumped off.

Perry let himself fall, spreading his hands. The birds descended after him like a pack of famished vultures after a scrap of meat. The wind blasted his face, clearing every trace of sleep from his eyes. Perry let Mew energy fill him till he could taste the power on the tip of his tongue. He heard the birds near him. He waited for them to get close. Then he transformed.

The blinding flash startled the raptors behind him. They dispersed in a ripple, thinking he had something planned. But he had nothing planned. He dove away from the apartment building and shot east along a street until he came to an intersection. He spun, beak pointed to the clouds, and put all power to his wings. He rarely flapped, because the winds just sort of gathered around his wings and pulled him in. However, now that he was running for his life, he flapped his more than three yards wide wings, ascending a great distance with each flap.

The seven raptors who had managed to keep up flapped feverishly, but couldn't match the rate of his climb. Still, Perry worried about the remaining that circled high above. If he made it past them, then there was no way they could get him. But if they managed to attack him before he got past their level, he might not make it. The Red Tails had proven that point.

Long before he reached the raptors above, Perry leveled off his ascent, and gathering the winds to his wings, he fired off eastward. He tilted upwards, slowly, as he raced across the heavens. The birds above and the birds below followed, angling in to converge on him. Perry immediately saw he had made a mistake. He couldn't avoid the convergence—it was too late. If he stopped, he'd lose speed and pay for it. *Maybe I could take advantage of the commotion somehow,* he thought.

The birds converged with a flurry of wings and glinting claws. Perry pulled in his wings and zipped through the convergence like a bullet. He veered left and right, missing talons and dagger-sharp beaks. He was almost through and would have made it had not a Red Tail caught him by his right shoulder with a well-aimed claw strike.

Pain shot through his mind like a javelin.

Perry was through, but he realized he was descending and losing speed. Pain had the effect of muddling his mind and keeping him from concentrating on flying. He felt a liquid substance escape his shoulders, trailing behind him. He spread his wings and felt a jolt of pain light up his senses. He bellied his wings back. Panic stabbed at his heart. If he could not fly, he was as good as dead.

Then the birds struck again.

It was the Red Tails' MO. They came in like lightning, striking and swerving away. After the third assault, Perry fell out of the air. The raptors weren't deterred. They came at him with more strikes that overloaded Perry's eagle's pain receptors. Perry felt like his body was an exposed wound with hot sauce sprinkled all over it. The ground, which looked like a coalescing of trees in his blurred vision, hurtled towards him.

Perry was now seconds away from crashing into the forest beneath. He spread his wing. The pain rushed his mind, and he let out a scream that came forth as a strange, shrill whistle. It sounded and felt more like a call for help than a cry of pain. The trees seemed to vibrate under the quickly spreading sound. He flapped once to slow his descent. He didn't get the chance to flap again. He crashed into the ground.

Perry hovered on the brink of unconsciousness. In his periphery, he could see a pack of raptors falling towards him, claws ready to deal out a deathly blow. Leading the attack were the Red Tails and the black falcon duo—Sarah's brothers.

Perry closed his eyes and flinched for impact.

There was none. Rather, he heard a gunshot. And then another. And another. Perry forced his eyes open and saw the birds fleeing in several different directions. He remained conscious long enough to see a man approach him, sling his gun around his back, and pick his aerial form up gently. Then everything went dark.

18

THE FORGER

Perry couldn't tell where he was when he finally came around. He was still in his eagle form, trapped in a massive cage sitting on a large oak table in a small cabin house. It was not their cabin house in the deserts of Nevada. It was a stranger's cabin house—a stranger who was sitting on a chair beside a workbench in the corner and working some sort of device.

Perry remained still, laying on his side, and scanned the small space, craning his neck to take in the whole room. It was clogged. Rays of sunlight leaked into the room through tiny holes. There was a wooden bed to the left, opposite the workbench. The table on which his cage stood was pulled up to the wall. Hanging on the walls were large scary masks. A pole like a totem stood in the corner. On the workbench, there were various curious tools: thin and precise. Also scattered around the small table were parts for a device. Perry couldn't tell what device.

Perry tried to pull himself to his legs, but pain shot through his nerves, and he whimpered.

The man raised his head from his work, paused his hands over the device, and turned to look at him. The man had grey hair, wrinkled face, and should have been old. But there was something about him. A vitality that sort of pulsed from him. Perry thought it strange.

The man's shoulders sagged. "You should rest, Eagle. You are badly injured."

Perry frowned. He thought he had heard that voice somewhere before. Also, he suspected that he must have thought the voice strange when he'd first heard it.

Perry tried to rise again, but his legs could not support his weight. They gave in with a flash of pain. This time Perry screamed—which came as a whistle—and blacked out. When he came around, it was dark outside. He knew this because he could not see any ray of sunlight filtering into the cabin. The old man was beside him, eating at the table. Perry's sense of smell in eagle form was poor, still, he could perceive the scrambled egg in the air.

Perry slowly swiveled his body on his ankles until he was staring at the man.

"If you want to get well, Eagle," the man said in a shrill, tired voice, "eat." He didn't look at Perry or stop eating.

Perry looked around his cage and saw a slab of cheese and a small bowl of water. He had never eaten in bird form before, but when he delved into the food, it came as second nature to him. He pecked little pieces off the cheese and ate. The food sort off frittered away into his belly. When the last piece was gone, he bent his beak into the bowl of water and sucked in. Naturally, the food wouldn't have satisfied him in human form. However, being an eagle, his stomach was smaller.

Perry tried to put a little weight on his legs. Though they still ached, they were now able to support him. He looked at his shoulder where a Red Tail had struck him. It had already healed remarkably, but it still throbbed with pain in the same way his wings and his underside throbbed. He was definitely healing. However, he feared he didn't know to what end. He remembered flying over a forest area before he fell. He had fallen into a reserve where birds were game, probably Inwood Hill Park.

Once the man finished his food, he left the plate on the table and retired to his wooden bed. The bed resisted his weight with loud creaks, but the man paid no attention to it. He fell into a deep slumber, one of soft snarls and snoring.

Perry settled on his legs. He breathed a sigh to relieve, the tension in his throat. And then, he went to sleep.

The next day, he felt stronger and grew more concerned. His parents were no doubt looking all over town for him. Or not—maybe they thought he was dead. Maybe, they were now mourning him. Each second Perry spent trapped in this house, his enemy—the sea monster—grew stronger. The task force had no idea how to kill the monster. Only he did. But he was trapped and may soon be dead, depending on what his captor wanted with an eagle. He knew that eagle skin was quite expensive. Or maybe he wanted to sell him to the zoo. Central Park would pay a lot for an eagle his size.

Perry watched as the man changed his clothes and left the house. He had dropped another slab of cheese in the cage and a fresh bowl of water before Perry had woken. Perry ate and drank and slept until the man returned hours later. When he opened the door, Perry got a peak outside. It was dark, but he saw outlines of trees and concluded that he was still on the reserve in Manhattan.

A thought came to him and he whistled. The whistle came through with a blast.

The man cringed back, his hands shooting to his ears. The whistle was stronger than Perry had intended, tearing through the room and shattering every glass.

"Stop that!" the man roared.

Perry reared and hit the other end of the cage.

The man was furious. His eyes seemed to light up. "No one can hear you, Eagle," he said. "You're all alone. One more whistle and that's it for you." The man went about his business as if Perry should have understood what he had said. *Eagles don't understand English, do they?*

Perry looked at his cage. It was barely large enough to turn to human form, although he would be tightly squeezed in if he did. Maybe, if the man saw he wasn't just another game, he would let him go. But that would go against the Mews most sacred rule. He couldn't reveal himself to an outsider.

The old man repeated his routine that night. He worked a long time on that device. Then he replaced Perry's food. They ate together in silence and fell asleep roughly at the same time.

The next day was the same boring cycle.

Perry was already restless. He was fully recovered. So he fluttered in the cage, making clattering noises with his claws. The day wore fast, and Perry found himself yet again at dinner with no clue who this man was or why he had him caged. When they had finished eating, the man dragged his chair to Perry's front and looked at him.

"Fear not, Eagle," the man said. "I will not kill you or sell you. Tomorrow, I will release you." Then the man sighed and bowed his head for a while. When he raised his head back up, he said, "What lies ahead of you is almost too much for one little hatchling to bear."

Perry caught his breath. *Hatchling* was a specific word used for new Mews not big sized raptors.

"Can one person handle so much chaos in our world?"

Perry cocked his head at the man. If by chaos he meant the sea monster, then yes, Perry could. Nonetheless, he was not alone. His friends, Sarah and James, would stand by him. But that was beside the point. Did this man really know about the Mews? The only way he could know about the Mewranters was if he was a Mew himself. If he was, then was he friend or foe? Perry was more inclined to believe he was a friend of their family because he hadn't killed him to absorb his power. He had saved Perry from a horrible death.

"Rest, Perry," the man said, and went over to his bed.

Perry remained still, astonished. He fell asleep sometime after the man was snoring.

♦ ♦ ♦

The sound of a vehicle driving up to their cabin woke Perry up. The man was already awake, dressed in a cream shirt and black pants. He grabbed a hold of Perry's cage by the head and pulled it off the table with great strain. He carried Perry out, descended two steps, and dumped him on his dusty yard. The brightness outside blinded him for a second. When his eyes adjusted, Perry recognized the car parking a few feet away. It was his family's battered pickup truck.

Mother jumped out of the car. She was dressed in a white gown, which fell short of her knees. She ran towards him, sliding to crouch before him. Both hands came through the iron bars and caressed his plumage. Perry purred like a kitten.

"Oh, my baby," she was saying, her face flushing with relief, "thank God you're safe."

"He's not going to stay that way if you don't act now, Joanna," the man barked.

Father came around. He knelt and ran his hand through Perry's feathers. Then he stood and approached the man. "You were vague over the phone three days ago," Father said to the man. "How did you say you found him?"

"I was drawn to him, Greg."

Perry felt his father stiffen. Mother's hands paused in his feathers.

"Felix, don't—"

"He called me, Greg," the man, Felix, said. "He called me to him. If he hadn't, the Red Tails and the Crofts would have finished him off."

"You're just trying to get us to lose our son," Father replied, incredulous.

"This is not about losing him, Greg," Felix said. "It's about saving his life."

"Look, Felix," Father said. "People are already afraid of him just for being an eagle. Now, you're telling me he has *the call*? What do you think would happen if people got to know he's not just an eagle, but that he's infinitely more powerful?"

"That's why you have to take him to The Forger," said Felix, matter-of-fact.

Greg shook his head. "No way."

"Tell me," Felix said, "what happened to the task force?"

Joanna stood and walked over to the duo. Perry turned so he could see the three.

"We were disbanded," Joanna replied. "Thank you, brother, for keeping an eye out for him until we could come over here without being followed."

"Yeah well, I've done my bit to protect the boy. But if you kids keep fooling around, he's going to end up dead, just like Jonathan."

That struck a chord in Mother. Grief poured out of her like a mighty river, bristling over Perry's feathers.

Greg scowled at Uncle Felix. "How dare you!?"

Felix ignored him and said to Mother, "Joanna, send him away,"— *send me away?*—"It's the only way he'll be free. What are you going to do? Take him back to your apartment? You'd all be slaughtered there. The sea, the land, the air, it's all being monitored. If his primal nature were let loose, he could make it away to the safety of a pack."

Perry didn't like the way that sounded. He didn't like the way the conversation was going.

Joanna began to sob. "I can't lose him, Felix. Not another son."

"It is better he's alive and safe somewhere else than dead in the ground, because if he stays, he's definitely going to be dead in the ground before long. The Mews are throwing their bodies against this monster to save the humans, Jo! The death count has become too much. This man-hunt for Perry will not cease until he is dead and gone."

Greg held Joanna in his hand. "We can fight. There are Mews who will stand by us."

"The Fortins?" Felix laughed wryly. "You want to start *another* re-bellion when the sea monster grows stronger each day with the blood of every slain Mew?" This seemed to anger Felix because he turned and started up his steps. On the porch, he looked back at them. "I warned you, Jo," he said, bitter. "I warned you about Jonathan. But you wouldn't listen. Please, listen now. Take him to see The Forger. Spare his life." He entered the cabin, shutting the door behind him.

Okay, Perry thought, *forget the crazy uncle. Let me go and we'll figure this out.*

Joanna broke the embrace. "Let's go."

She entered the car while Father, instead of releasing Perry, trans-ferred his cage into the trunk. The cage was too big to fit into the car. Perry was confused and scared. He fluttered in the cage but was ignored by his parents. Father got into the car and began to drive.

There was a silence in the vehicle.

After close to three hours of driving, they got to a junction where the road turned left and a dirt path started right, hedged in by tall grasses. Father parked in the middle of the road.

"Joanna," he said, "have you made your decision?"

She nodded. "Let's go to The Forger."

Perry could feel his father's fear spiking. He swallowed hard. "Joanna—"

"I've decided, Greg. To The Forger. Let's not make this harder than it already is."

Greg nodded and guided the car unto the dirt strip. They took three more turns and drove for thirty more minutes before they came to a lone building. It was a needle-like structure rising at least seven stories into the air. Like their cabin in Nevada, the structure seemed to have been constructed solely from roofing sheets. It shouldn't have been standing, laws of physics and all. But then, Perry shouldn't be able to turn into an eagle, either.

When they parked, a medium height, average age man dressed in a brown night robe ran out of the building through a door that Perry had not seen.

"No, no, no, no!" he wailed. "Not you two. Go away!"

Father got out of the car. "Yeah, Jude. Nice to see you, too."

Joanna stepped down from the vehicle. "We need your help, J," she said. "We need to send Perry away."

Perry heard it and a loud gong went off in his mind. Fear got a hold of him and gripped tightly.

Father hefted the cage out of the truck and set it on the ground. Jude bent to examine him, eyes flickering between curiosity and total awe.

"Look at the size of that thing," he muttered. "Bigger than any Mew I've ever seen. Amazing."

"J!" Mother snapped.

Jude jerked up. He cleared his throat. "I'm afraid I'm going to have to decline, Jo. The Central Council has issued a directive to all Forgers. Perry, the eagle, cannot be fitted with any brace."

Joanna nodded, a slight smile forming at the corner of her lips. It didn't go further. "Your decline has been noted. Now move along."

Jude stared at her for a while, unsure what to do next. Then, he grunted and led the way. "Bring him inside."

Jo followed. Father lifted the cage and limped into the needle house. The building wasn't divided into floors. It was hollow all the way to the roof at which point the walls converged in a small port. Large balconies circled the walls at several points along the length of the building. They walked a narrow path to a winding staircase and continued upwards. As they ascended, Perry got a better look at the inside. There were giant machines clogging the hollow structure. These machines gave off noise similar to the noise bottling machines gave off. Perry didn't know anything about machines, so he couldn't tell what their uses were.

They came to the topmost balcony.

"Drop him on that table," Jude said, rummaging through a stack of books on a shelf farther down the balcony.

Father dropped the cage on a table near the wall. He stood there transfixed on Perry. Mother was facing a contraption in the wall. It looked like a holder for something. Something as large as his cage. There was a long and wide door in the wall.

When Jude returned, he was holding a metal shackle and wearing a long face. "I'm sorry, Jo. But this is what I have now."

"Where will it take him?" she asked.

"The Fire Breathers in the north," came the reply.

"Blasted Felix!" Greg exploded. "He planned this." His eyes narrowed on Jude. "Did he put you up to this?"

Jude took a step back, shaking his head. "I think it's a bad idea, too. Give me seven days and I'll make you another brace."

Joanna had turned away. She was now facing Perry, looking at him with tired eyes. "No one can make a brace within seven days. Even if you could, Perry does not have seven days. Put the brace on him."

A look of surprise came on Greg's and Jude's faces.

"Are you sure about that?" Jude asked. "I mean, their acceptance process can be really brutal."

Joanna scoffed. "That's putting it mildly, Jude. But at least he'll be among his kind."

Greg took a hold of Joanna's hands and pulled her to the side, away from earshot. Perry heard perfectly.

"Jo, reconsider this," he said. "We don't have to send him away. We can smuggle him to Africa to stay with my family there."

"And risk an all-out war amongst our kind?" Joanna replied. "That's too much for the life of one person."

"He's our son, Jo," Greg said, firm.

"And I love him," Joanna replied. "But he's safer away from us than with us. We tried to hide with Jonathan. It failed. I'm not going to lose Perr, too, Greg."

"What do you call handing him over to the Fire Breathers in the north?" Greg asked. "He's too young and utterly inexperienced to handle their initiation process."

"But think of it," Joanna said with a twinge of excitement in her voice. "If he survives, he'll be formidable and that would only be the beginning. Many would rally to his cause. He'd rule as a scepter of justice over all Mews everywhere. It would be a new dawn for our kind."

"You forget something, Jo," Greg said. "That brace Jude has in his hands is never coming off. It's a banishment brace. He's never coming back."

Joanna looked over her shoulder at Perry. Perry squirmed.

"Put the brace on him, J," Joanna commanded.

Perry lost a handle on his emotions. He panicked and fluttered out of control.

"Don't you want to say goodbye?" Jude drew closer to the cage, oblivious to Perry's sudden outburst.

"If we let him go, J, he'll run away."

"No. I meant you transforming and saying goodbye."

Joanna considered it. A longing appeared in her eyes for a moment. Then she shook her head. "It'll be too hard for both of us. It's better this way."

Jude turned, and with blinding speed, he caught a hold of Perry's leg. Before Perry could bring his free leg along with its sharp end to bear on the hand, the cold metal brace clamped around his leg.

A jolt like electricity shot through him. A bout of spasms wrenched his body.

Mother and Father stood by, watching. Perry felt himself slip off the reins of command. He felt himself fall to the background as another personality took the floor. He watched helplessly as his body calmed and settled on its talons under the command of another. For a brief moment, everything lost meaning. But it didn't stay that way because he soon remembered who he was. He was Eagle.

Eagle wondered where he was. Who was the man in the strange apparel, the one that had touched him? If it weren't for the cage, he would have torn the man to pieces for setting his filthy hands on his body. Who were the man and woman behind him, looking at him strangely as if he were naked? Only one thing made sense to Eagle. He had to fly to the northern Eagle Tribe. He didn't know why. But as soon as he got out of this cage, that was where he was headed.

"It's done," the one that had touched him said. He carried the cage and placed it on the contraption in the wall, aligning the door of the cage with the door in the wall. The man looked at the couple. "You don't have to go through with this," he said. "You can still save him."

"Set him loose, J," the woman said. "He's already gone."

The man called J pressed a green button on the wall. There was a sound. The door began to rise up and up until there was nothing separating Eagle from the vast blue sky. In the blink of an eye, Eagle sprung for the opening. Immediately, his wings came free, massive as they were, carrying him beyond the top of the building. Just as he broke through the first layer of clouds, he sensed danger.

19

EAGLE JOURNEYS TO THE ARCTIC CIRCLE

The danger was still miles away, coming in fast from the west as a numerous company of lesser raptors. Eagle snickered at their impudence. Didn't they know he was Eagle? He would lay waste to them today. Eagle was already moving too fast for them, though he was moving in the wrong direction. Somehow, he knew he couldn't stay to fight. But when he changed direction, his new heading would bring him into contact with at least seven of the raptors. *That is enough to make a statement, Eagle thought excitedly.*

He veered off his current path and headed north. The raptors closed in on him fast. Eagle, without craning his neck, espied his victims. Two red-tailed kites, four hawks, and a falcon. The two Red Tails were descending on him from on high. They thought they had the advantage; Eagle *let* them think they had the advantage. Them, he would kill.

The falcon came in first, zipping headlong into him. Eagle, at the last moment, shot up, picking the bird by its neck. One squeeze of his claws, and he felt the rush of blood from the raptor's neck. The falcon wriggled, cried out, and fell off Eagle's hook—lifeless—towards land. The hawks were lucky because they came at him with a higher speed. He caught one by the leg, slammed it into another, and beaked yet another in the eye. The fourth pulled off its dive before it could get to him.

Already, Eagle could see the remaining birds calling off their attack. However, the Red Tails still came. Eagle's heart drummed with excitement. If he were any of the other lesser raptors, Eagle should have been disadvantaged. But he wasn't a lesser raptor. He was the most powerful bird alive. He was an eagle.

Eagle spun with striking speed such that when the first Red Tail came into range, it met his extended claws. Eagle caught hold of the startled bird's neck and snapped it. Before the other Red Tail could respond, Eagle was ripping its chest until he saw its pumping heart. Though the Red Tail was already dead by now, he still thrust his bloodied claws into the heart cavity and pulled out the organ.

Eagle continued north, two lifeless bodies and a heart dropping to the earth beneath him. He didn't know exactly where he was going. All he knew was that he had to continue north. When he got to his destination, he wouldn't feel the need to travel. But now, he had to travel.

Eagle traveled for days. Eagle didn't travel in the night because his eyesight was poor in the dark. So every night, he found shelter and rested. Where there was no shelter, he built one. He built nests in the highest places. For the first four days, he built nests in those giant man-made buildings. Finding the sticks he needed was difficult. So was transferring the sticks from ground level to the site of construction. But Eagle did it.

Feeding was exciting as much as it was nourishing. He fed on rats and rabbits and birds. After the fourth day, he rarely saw any human settlement. Everything turned white and got bone-chilling cold. His feathers developed icicles. He flew through snow storms. Shelter was scarce. But Eagle had to get to his destination. The fifth and sixth days were the hardest. On the sixth day, he flew low, close to the ground. So if he fainted out of exhaustion, he wouldn't be too badly injured. The whole expansive landscape was covered in snow and ice, devoid of life. Not a thing moved.

As the day stretched, Eagle came to a lake. It was vast with no end in sight to it. From afar, Eagle could already see many moving things beneath its surface. His already ailing heart pumped once more with vigor. The dizziness cleared from his eyes as his body gave him its final strength to feed. Eagle swung into the air and, like a projectile, shot towards the surface of the water. His claws made contact with the icy water between one moment and the next.

He soared around and headed inland. He dropped the fish far away from the lake. He headed back to the sea. Three cycles, and he had enough fishes for a feast. He tore the fishes apart till the bones lay scattered on the ice. A beak down in the lake for a satisfying gulp, and he had his strength back. Immediately, he was high up in the clouds again, heading north. That day, he found an abandoned human outpost.

Early the next day, just before dawn, Eagle was already flying. He hadn't flown for most of the morning when he was attacked. They were as large as he was. Eagles. Eagle stood no chance. Before he saw the first bird, he was already surrounded. They approached him from both high up and down below, giving him no space to maneuver. The first bird, a black eagle, had its claw stretched to attack. Eagle met it with his own claws, but before he could do any other thing, other claws had tightened around his wings and shoulders from above. He had been picked out of the air.

Eagle wriggled and whistled. But this only served to tighten the eagles' grips on him.

There were tens of other eagles in the attack party. They flew on north until they got to an ice mountain. They flew in through a small opening. Once through, the attack party disbanded. Only five, including the two that had his wings clipped, continued straight. The innards of the mountain were considerably warmer than outside. It was a network of ice nests spreading in every direction. There must have been hundreds of eagles here, all as big as he was.

The eagles watched with sneering gazes as he was carried through. Some left their nests and followed.

Eagle was thrown into an empty nest. One that was constructed within a wall, having one unbarricaded opening, which functioned as both an entrance and an exit. The moment his wings were free, Eagle sprung into the air. He didn't make it past one yard before he was struck by lightning—*no!*—by the black bird that had initiated the attack on him earlier. It slashed Eagle's wings. Eagle lost his surge of energy, falling back into his prison.

The black bird hovered just outside the nest, its dark eyes burning through Eagle's body. "*The next time you try to escape,*" its hard voice resounded in Eagle's mind. "*It'll be your neck.*" Then, it ascended and was gone.

Beyond his nest birds were perching on nests in their hundreds, all watching him and murmuring. There were five nests that stood out, high above his. They were empty at first and different. They were separated from the rest, like a judge's seat was separate from the audience's in a courtroom. Five eagles perched on these five nests after a while. The assembly fell silent.

Eagle envied these birds. They were beautiful and graceful. Jet black, crimson red, lime green, snow white, and sky blue; these birds stood tall, wings stretched. The result was a murmur from the gathered eagles.

"*May justice prevail,*" they sang, their voices a sonorous melody.

The birds bellied their wings.

"*State your name and purpose for being here, Eagle,*" the one in the middle, the white one, said. Eagle could sense the revulsion in his voice.

"*My name is Eagle,*" Eagle said. But deep down, he knew he used to go by another name. Something that started with the letter 'P.'

The eagles snorted, but they didn't press.

"*Why have you come to us, Eagle?*" This one came from the yellow eagle. It was a female.

"*I do not know,*" Eagle replied. "*I lived trapped among the humans until I was set free and had the urge to come here.*"

A murmur swept the gathering. Something was wrong.

"*So you are a Mew?*" The red one asked. But he already knew the answer to that because it was more of a statement than a question.

Now, Eagle didn't know what a Mew was. But he knew somehow that the one whose name began with 'P' was a Mew. But that could have been him, *or was him*. It was just too confusing.

"*Yes, I am,*" Eagle replied anyway.

"*There is only one reason,*" the green bird said, preempting the murmur that was starting in the back, "*why Mew eagles come here, Eagle. To be tried. Is that why you have come?*"

For lack of what to say, Eagle said, "*Yes.*" He was up to any trial.

"*What insolence,*" the middle bird roared, spitting fire from his mouth. At that same moment, the edge of his wings metamorphosed into sharp metal. He rose to his full stature. The fire now sputtered and caused him to cough. "*You would dare come here to be tried, you insolent hatchling?!*" His voice in Eagle's mind was a deep bellow.

"*He shall be executed,*" the red bird said in support.

Eagle stood his ground, though his legs shivered from fear.

"*Let us not rush into a decision,*" the yellow, female bird said, calm. "*After all, he is a Mew and he is called. Little wonder we can communicate so fluidly.*"

The black bird gave a throaty laugh. His eyes narrowed on Eagle. "*We heard your call, Eagle,*" he said in a taunting voice "*You called us, and we failed to come to your aid. You are not worthy of our powers, Eagle. You are incompetent, unlearned, and rash. You will never be tried."*

Eagle didn't know why it should, but the black eagle's statement enraged him. Eagle took two quick steps to the open doorway of his prison, intent on attacking the bird. Two birds dropped suddenly into view from above and hovered in the doorway. Eagle retreated, and they ascended out of view.

The black bird scowled at Eagle, turning to his fellows. *"He shall be executed at dawn for his insolence. Any objections?"*

No bird objected. Eagle's fate was sealed.

The leader turned back to Eagle. He opened his beak to speak, but words came from somewhere else.

"He shall not be executed!" It was strong, authoritative, and strangely familiar.

A red, blue, and white phoenix flew into view and perched on an empty nest a little to the right below the five. *"The trial is a test of worthiness for every Mew bird that makes it to this pack. It is not for worthy eagles. It is to* make *worthy eagles. It cannot be decided by this assemble who is tried or who is not. Beulah! Call yourself to order."*

A soft murmur washed over the gathering.

The black bird looked as if he had been bashed in the face. He glared at the phoenix, who was several inches shorter, though still Mew large. He said nothing in reply.

The phoenix continued. *"The Mews now face the greatest threat we have ever faced. One that, if allowed to prevail, will kill every creation of good. Including this pack. Yet, you seek to execute our only hope?"*

The black eagle who had now settled in his nest scoffed aloud. *"Look not for hope in this one, Phoenix. Even if we don't kill him, he will never survive the trial. Never. Do not forget that our redemption has been promised by so many eagle Mews for over a thousand years. Eagles that were champions of causes—heroes in their worlds—and yet failed miserably at the trial. Do you not think that we have had enough heartbreaks already?"*

"This one is different, Beulah."

"This one will fail!" Black bellowed. He mellowed and said, *"If he is our only hope, then do not insist he be tried."*

"I insist, Beulah." The phoenix stared the eagle down.

Beulah heaved a sigh. *"Then, so be it. The trial shall begin at dawn."*

"One more thing," the phoenix said. *"The eagle came here by a banishment brace. If he is to stand a chance at winning, he must fight not only with power but also with personality."*

"You request we take off the brace?" Beulah asked with an incredulous smile. *"Subjecting the eagle to the man will reduce his chances of winning, especially when the man has not yet mastered his aerial form."* Beulah paused, considering the matter. *"Very well. His brace may be removed. But two guards shall watch over him lest he attempts to escape. This assembly is dismissed."*

It started as a whisper and developed through murmurs until becoming a noise. The birds dispersed. In the flurry of activity, the phoenix landed in the doorway of the prison. *"Eagle,"* it started to say, but it was interrupted by the black bird who had caught Eagle earlier.

"Step aside, Phoenix," the black eagle said. Two other formidable eagles—one grey, the other ash—hovered behind him.

The phoenix stepped inside, moving to the side. *"This is going to be a shock,"* he said as black, grey, and ash entered the small cave. Eagle lashed out, but grey and ash were faster, clamping him down on the icy floor. Before his eyes, the edges of the hovering black bird's wings transformed to metal. They were dagger sharp.

The bird descended on Eagle, bringing down the sharp ends of its wings on Eagle's leg. There was a loud clang. The heavy metal bracket around his leg fell as two parts.

A flood of images besieged Eagle's mind. He blacked out.

20
UNCLE FELIX, THE PHOENIX

P erry woke with a definite headache, though it wasn't the headache that woke him. He felt something poke at his legs: sharp,
cold, and hard. His whole body was freezing, yet, he did not
know if it was his eagle body or his human body.

"*You think he's going to wake up, Dan?*" one voice, cool as the floor,
said. "*Yates hit him pretty hard.*"

There was another poke on his leg. It was stronger and the claws
pierced deeper. Perry stiffened reflexively. The thing, whatever it was,
scampered back.

"*Looks like it, Bran,*" another voice said. "*He must be a very dumb
Mew. He managed to piss off Yates and Beulah on the same day.*"

Images of his encounter began to come back to him in a kaleidoscopic flood of pain. His parents had pushed him away, abandoned
him. They had exiled him. Perry's heart began to burn with grief. Tears
formed in his eyes and fell down his beak. He opened his eyes. A wall
of ice stood in front of him. He was lying on his belly in a prison some-

where in the Arctic Circle. He had eaten rats and rabbits and had lived in nests and unwholesome places. He felt dirty, rotten, and sad.

"*Yo, Eagle,*" the one with the cool and scary voice, Bran, said. "*Are you going to lie on your belly all day?*" He certainly had no regard or respect for him, Perry could tell.

Perry moaned, his head throbbing. "*If I have to, yes,*" he muttered to the eagles behind him.

One of them chuckled. "*Well forgive me for noticing, Eagle,*" Dan said, "*but you have a trial to prepare for tomorrow!*"

"*My name is not Eagle,*" Perry said, using his wings to turn on his belly so he faced the eagles. "*My name is Perry Johnson.*"

One was huge and muscular, while the other was smaller and thinner. The muscular one was dark grey and had silver linings in his facial plumage, whereas the other one was brown like Perry and had a white circlet in his neck area. They both stood guard at the entrance.

"*Well, Perry,*" the muscular eagle, Bran, said, "*die at the trial tomorrow or die now.*" He took one claw step forward.

"*Might as well die now,*" Dan suggested. "*We'll make it quick and painless. That's way better than what awaits you north of here.*"

Perry remembered the events of earlier today. He began to feel his belly turn. He looked around, beyond the open doorway, considering an escape. The nests beyond the prison were deserted. In fact, Perry couldn't see another eagle save these two with him. Maybe they had gone hunting for food or something. If he could get past these two guards, he could make a quick escape.

Bran stood over him, his claws glinting in Perry's face. "*Go ahead,*" he said, his dark eyes looking down at Perry with indignation. "*Give me a reason.*"

Perry tried to move, but his wings and leg still hurt badly. He felt a pressure in his throat.

"*Yes,*" Dan said, now beside Bran, "*give us a reason.*"

A shape filled the doorway. "*Stop it, you two!*" It was a female. She leaped into the air and landed on the two, smacking her wings into their heads. They scampered away from her, retreating to the entrance. She gently laid a small plate she held in her beak near Perry. She turned to the two birds who now hung their heads in shame. She glared at them, her eyes startling flames of fire.

Perry gazed up at her and felt his eagle drawn to her. Her wings were a mix of scarlet and wine. Her tail was white, which matched the red of her head. She turned away from the two.

"*Sorry, Eagle,*" she said with a soft, sweet voice. "*My brothers can be really...zesty.*" She threw another icy glare at them. They cringed backwards.

Perry relaxed, more from her soothing voice than from her ability to control the two eagles. "*My name is Perry.*"

"*Hi, Perry,*" she said with a smile. Or at least he thought it was a smile. "*My name is Noniella. You've already met my brothers, Bran and Dan. Beulah is our father.*"

"*Great!*" Perry whined. "*The one that wanted to have me executed without a chance.*"

Noniella ignored his remark. Using her beak, she picked up a small cloth from the plate and placed it on his leg, where it hurt. Perry saw that a red scar had already developed there. The cloth was chilly, sending shivers through his body. But after the sting of cold, the pain began to subside until it was gone.

"*Is it good?*" she asked.

"*Yes, actually,*" Perry replied. "*What is that stuff?*"

She removed the cloth from his legs, placing it back on the plate. It soaked the liquid.

"*It's a healing potion,*" Noniella replied. She placed the cloth on his left wing. The pains there dissipated. Then she placed it on his other wing. When she was done, Perry wasn't feeling any pain anywhere. He, however, still felt weak.

"You got anything for weakness?" Perry asked. He meant it as a joke, but she took it seriously.

Noniella glanced at him. "*Seek not what makes you stronger, but what makes you wiser, Perry.*"

"*Oh,*" Perry replied.

"*Stand,*" she instructed him, taking several steps back.

Bran and Dan stood alert in case he should try to escape.

Perry slowly rose to his feet and spread his wings three yards wide on both sides. They simply stared at him. If he had done that before any Mew, they would have cringed or been amazed. Noniella moved around him, examining every inch of his body.

She ended up in his face. "*You seem to be all right.*" Then she smiled. "*There are no potions for body weakness, Perr. A good night sleep should fix you up.*"

Perry was taken aback by her statement. *Sarah and James,* he thought. He had to let them know he was still alive. He wondered what his parents had told them. He had to get out of here.

"*Where's everybody?*" Perry motioned to the empty nests beyond his door. "*The whole place looks deserted.*"

"*This is a small part of the mountain,*" she replied. "*There are caves like this along the wall. Usually, this is where defaulters are tried and sentenced.*"

"*Like a courtroom,*" Perry said.

"*What's that?*"

"*Never mind.*"

There was silence.

"*Phoenix has requested your presence,*" Noniella said at last. "*Bran and Dan will take you to his shelter.*" She clawed over to the door. "*Be nice to him,*" she said to them. "*He's far from home. Do this right and maybe Father will restore your positions in the royal army.*"

"*Yes, Sister,*" they replied, heads bowed.

"*Bye, Perry,*" Noniella said to him, leaped out the cave, and flew away.

Perry drew near to the door. "*Take me to see Phoenix.*"

They nodded and flew out the cave. Perry followed them. It was a hazard finding the exit. There were hundreds of eagles in flight. There were webs and overlapping webs of nests that they were constantly ducking and veering from. For Dan and Bran it seemed like routine, but Perry was constantly alert. The whole place vibrated with life. Birds tweeting, chirpy, whistling.

They were through after several minutes, bursting out through a hole in the mountainside. The cold air blasted through Perry's body with frigid intensity. The depressing snowy landscape replaced the lively inside of the mountain. They soared through the skies for a good hour before they came upon an RV. Bran whistled twice and the door to the RV opened. A man stepped out into the cold, looking up. It was Perry's uncle, Felix.

"*Go on,*" Dan said. "*We'll keep an eye on you from up here.*"

"*Thanks, guys,*" Perry said, and descended towards the vehicle. He transformed seamlessly several yards away and approached Felix.

Uncle Felix smiled. "Quickly, kid," he said, waving his hands into his caravan. "Don't want you to die before tomorrow now, do we?"

Perry followed him into the vehicle.

The place was warm and congested. A small bed took up the whole front part of the camper. A workbench filled the back, and a counter connected the bed to the bench. Above it was a shelf stocked with food. There were two chairs in the center.

Felix directed him to one of the chairs. Perry sat and watched his uncle.

Uncle Felix poured him a hot mug of chocolate milk. "You must be hungry," he said, retrieving a packet of wafers from the shelf. He poured some into a plate and handed it to Perry. Then, he sat in the other chair and watched Perry devour the food. Two other mugs of hot chocolate and three packets of wafers later, Perry was ready to listen to the man.

"You must have a lot of questions," he said. "But listen to all I have to say first. I believe as I talk, some of your questions will be answered."

"Are you really my uncle?" Perry blurted.

Uncle Felix didn't really like that interruption, but he answered anyway. "Yes. Joanna is my younger sister."

"Okay," Perry quipped, relishing the hot thick feel of the chocolate on his tongue. Food had a way of elevating Perry's mood.

"A lot of things have changed since you left Manhattan seven days ago, Perry," Uncle Felix said. "The task force was a massive failure. There have been deaths both to Man and Mew. With each drop of Mew blood spilled into the sea, the sea monster grows stronger and more formidable. As of now, the sea monster is the strongest it has ever been."

"Why?" Perry asked, angry. "Because they've not been able to kill me?"

"Because no eagle Mew since the spawning of the sea monster has ever lived this long without having to deal with the creature someway or the other," Uncle Felix replied. "The government has begun to respond to these human deaths. Every harbor and port along the Upper New York Bay, Hudson River, and East River has been closed. The beaches are closed. The local prices of all seafood have skyrocketed. People are scared of going near water."

Perry's mood became foul with each word.

Uncle Felix's voice quietened. "Just before you left, there was a rebellion. The Croft brothers led this rebellion against the Central Council. A death sentence was passed on your head. To every Mew, it was either kill you or be killed by the sea monster. But I and your parents and some elite Mews sensed it was not really the will of the people. The Crofts are using an evil power to bend people's minds. That's why your clan chief sent his son to warn you."

"Mr. Monte?"

Uncle Felix nodded, his intense gaze never once leaving Perry's face. He was judging Perry's reaction, measuring every expression. "When the task force failed to kill the monster and you were attacked at your home and nearly killed, the only other option was to send you away." He sighed with regret. "It was the hardest thing I've ever seen your mother do. It tore her apart, watching you die to your eagle."

Guilt welled up to Perry's throat. He had wrongly thought that his parents abandoned him. They only did it to save him.

"Uncle," Perry said, face down, "I think I killed some of those birds that attacked me..." His voice faltered as he recalled the incidence.

Uncle Felix nodded. "It wasn't you, Perr," he replied. "It was your eagle defending itself. Just after that your parents were seized, tried, and sentenced."

Perry looked up with a jerk. That caused the tears to fall free from his eyes. "What's the sentence?"

Uncle Felix paused. He seemed to be considering whether to tell him or not. "They are going to be sacrificed to the sea monster five days from now."

That gong went off again in Perry's mind. Perry was standing without even knowing it.

"Sit down, Perry," Uncle Felix said. "Settle down."

"How can I sit down, Uncle?" Perry was now pacing the small space. "It took me seven days to get here. How can I get back in time to save them?"

"The only way to save your parents is to kill the monster," Uncle Felix said.

Perry stopped and looked at his uncle. "I already know how to kill the blasted monster. I have to leave now! Maybe if I fly day and night, I can get there in time." Perry finally sat down because he was tired.

"Perry," Uncle Felix said, "it's not enough to know how to kill it. You need strength. You need power—you need all the help you can get. And here is the place you can get that help."

Perry stared at the man. "Are you referring to the trial?"

Uncle Felix beamed. "All hope is not lost yet—"

"You planned this, didn't you?" Perry asked. "You suggested this to my parents and they didn't like it."

"I didn't plan anything, Perr," he replied. "I just took advantage of a situation. You had a death tag on your back already. The only solution was to release your eagle and send you here."

Perry snorted. "What's this trial about anyway?"

"It's a test."

"What does it test?"

Uncle Felix sucked in a lungful of air and slowly breathed it out. "Follow me," he said and led Perry outside. They carried their chairs to the back of the van where there were sticks arranged to make a fire. Perched on top of the van in the dark were two ice statues. Bran and Dan.

Uncle Felix whistled with his tongue and they shook themselves and looked alive.

"Hey, boys," Uncle Felix called to them. "Some fire, would you?"

"*Get yourself a lighter, Phoenix,*" Bran called back, his voice filling Perry's mind, though he was in human form.

"Please, you two." Felix seemed to have heard as well.

They grumbled a bit before flapping over to the wood. When they breathed deep, their chests turned to gleeds. Then, they blasted the wood. Perry expected to see a flood of fire but what came out were sparks of flames and sputters. It was enough to set the fueled wood ablaze.

"Thank you," Uncle Felix said and sat down. Perry drew his chair closer to the fire. The birds landed near the flame and warmed themselves in its glow. Darkness had already settled upon the landscape.

"To understand the trial," Uncle Felix said, "you must first understand why it exists. Its origin.

"Once in these lands, there existed a nation of eagles called The Fire Breathers. They were large birds whose wings became sharp metallic spikes that could cut metal with a stroke. But, their defining quality was their ability to spit fire like dragons. They aided the Mews in their battle against evil till they lost that which was precious to them."

Uncle Felix rubbed his hands near the fire.

"What did they lose?"

"*We lost our flag,*" Dan replied, fidgeting on the cold ground. His claws were not getting the same warm treatment as his feathers and body.

"You lost a flag?"

"*It's not just any flag, Perry,*" Bran replied. "*It's our symbol. It's what unites us—our identity. If we have no identity, we have no power.*"

Perry turned from the bird and faced Uncle Felix, who was watching him. "So, when they lost the flag, they lost their fire-breathing ability."

Uncle Felix nodded. "They lost their strength, their fire-breathing ability, and their metallic wings. What you saw demonstrated by a few of them is merely a residual effect. One that is quickly fading away."

Perry realized then what the trial was all about. "You want me to retrieve the flag?"

"*Yes,*" Bran and Dan echoed at the same time. Uncle Felix merely nodded.

Perry frowned. "But, these eagles have powerful people among themselves. Why can't any of them get the flag? Why does it have to be me?"

"Because these eagles were never born to be a self-sustaining unit. They were born to follow an eagle Mew. That's what the call is about. Every thousand years, an eagle comes along who has the ability to summon this pack of eagles to war."

Perry's eyes widened. "That's what you were talking about with Father? I have the call?"

Uncle Felix nodded. "That was why I could help you when you needed help. That whistle was a call. And because I'm a part of this pack, I had to respond."

"But, I whistled just a few seconds before I crashed into the trees. You couldn't have made it to me in time had you heard the call when I whistled."

"I was following you, Perry. I could feel your distress. I had a general idea where you were. When you whistled, I was already close by to respond."

"Beulah said something about hearing the call and failing to respond. That I was not worthy."

Uncle Felix sighed. "The Fire Breathers will not follow you until you prove yourself to them. The reason I helped you wasn't because you called. It was because you're my nephew."

Perry's heart warmed. "So," he breathed, "I simply have to go to this trial, retrieve the flag, and the eagles will follow me to battle?"

Bran scoffed. "*Only if it were that easy.*"

"Perry, the trial is dangerous," Uncle Felix said. "It is anything but simple and you run the risk of losing your life out there. But, yes. Retrieve the flag and not only will the eagles follow you to their deaths, you'll also inherit their strength, fire, and metallic wings."

Before Perry could get excited about the prospects of being able to spit fire like a dragon, Uncle Felix added, "Many have died in the trial, Perry. It is not a game. Only three eagles have ever survived the trial. Pranis, your ancestor, was one of them. He had the call just like you, which is why I know you're capable of surviving the trial."

"Hold on," Perry said. "If Pranis succeeded, why is there still a trial?"

"With the death of each eagle successor, the flag disappears and returns to the valley and we lose our powers," Dan said, solemn. His claws had adapted to the icy ground and were now rooted deep.

"It's like a curse," Bran added. *"We are bound to this vicious cycle."*

There was silence.

"Perry, no one knows the true nature of the trial. Only that there are five tests that are designed to test you as an individual." Uncle Felix drew closer to Perry and dropped his voice. Perry had no illusion that the eagles couldn't hear what Uncle Felix said. "You can escape now, Perry. Bran and Dan won't stop you—"

"Don't be too sure of that, Phoenix," Dan's high pitch voice intruded.

"—or you can stay here. The trial is the only way we can defeat the sea monster once and for all. But beyond that, it is one of the only ways we can survive the darkness that is about to befall the earth. You must know this by now. Evil nature is rising in power."

Perry remained quiet, gazing into the fire. The air was still and frigid, but Perry was kept warm by the blazing fire. If he agreed to the trial, he would probably die. But if he didn't do it, he may not be able to defeat the sea monster. Perry recalled his former "average" life. He had always lived life in the shadows, in the middle, in the class of the average. Turning into the eagle had changed a lot of things for him. People looked up to him. People expected him to be a solution and to save his people. He couldn't afford to be average any longer.

Perry knew that his one-way ticket out of average was the trial. It would give him the strength and abilities he needed to defeat the sea monster and face other threats that were surely coming.

Perry squeezed his eyes shut and focused his attention on his pounding heart. Dawn was close. Death might be closer. The trial was the only way forward.

"I'll do it, Uncle," Perry said, opening his eyes. "I'll do it."

Uncle Felix nodded. He barely said much after this. Perry conversed with Bran and Dan until midnight when Uncle Felix instructed him to go inside and sleep. Perry cozied up under thick blankets in the RV. He was still nervous and anxious, but he was no longer scared. *It will turn out right*, he told himself. *It will turn out right.*

21

THE VALLEY OF DEATH

Uncle Felix woke Perry before dawn.

Perry stirred, tiny electric currents running through his bones. Uncle Felix offered him some food, but Perry rejected it. He couldn't eat in this state. He was much too antsy for food. Perhaps, he wasn't hungry. The way he felt was similar to how he had felt earlier last week when he found out about the family ritual. Only, in this case, he wasn't dealing with expulsion from the fold; he was dealing with death. That wasn't comforting.

Perry sat on the bed for a while watching Uncle Felix do unnecessary chores. He cleaned already cleaned plates and arranged already arranged clothes. He too was anxious. It was bad for Perry. At least one of them was supposed to be the brave one.

Perry jumped off the bed and his feet touched the cold floor. The room was warm even though Perry could hear a blizzard raging outside. He slogged over to the counter and took a glass of water.

"Are you sure you don't want any food?" Uncle Felix asked. His eyes were tired; his face was tight with tension. Perry could tell he hadn't gotten much sleep last night. Probably worrying over him, Perry thought.

"No, Uncle," Perry replied, placing the tumbler on the counter. He felt groggy. It wasn't everyday he got to sleep without dreaming about the sea monster. Nevertheless, just because the sea monster didn't show up in his dreams didn't mean he got to sleep well. Perry must have woken up twenty times in the past six hours. No sea monster in his dreams, but thoughts of what lay ahead of him today was as good as the sea monster when it came to a night's rest.

There was a *tak-tak-tak* sound on the roof of the vehicle. Perry recognized it as claws tapping the metallic roof. Uncle Felix stiffened at the sound, turning to face Perry. His eyes told him it was time.

Perry was trying to calm himself, to expunge the tension building in his blood. But Uncle Felix wasn't making it easy; he was infecting Perry with his worried gazes and gesticulations. Perry pulled his sneaker from under the bed where he had shoved it last night. He tightened the straps around his feet and straightened up. He still had on the clothes he had worn before they were attacked at the house. It was a grey sweatshirt and jeans.

He heaved a sigh to reduce the pressure in his chest and motioned to the door. "Are we going or what?"

Uncle Felix opened the door and led Perry into the deathly cold outside. The blizzard was still ravaging the white landscape. It took Perry's eyes quite some time to adjust. When they did, he saw the company that had come to take him to the trial. Several yards away from the van, the five birds—leaders of the pack—had their claws and beaks facing the ice; their wings surrounding their body. Behind them there were about ten black eagles. Perry recognized Yates, who stood directly behind Beulah. Then behind them, spread all the way to the back, must have been over one hundred Mew-large eagles of different colors.

Uncle Felix bent into Perry. "They have come to pay their respects. It's not every time an eagle Mew comes along to try and free them."

"Yeah," Perry replied, scanning the ranks of eagles, "I can guess why." He spotted Bran and Dan on the fourth row to the left. Instead of bowing in respect, they waved their wings at him. He smiled and waved back.

After a while, Beulah raised his head. On cue, all the other birds raised their heads in a silent fluid motion. Hundreds of pairs of eyes gazed at him. Perry gazed back with his hands clenched. He could see the hope in their eyes. Some of them wanted to believe that he could save them. They were desperate.

Perry realized with a shock that he wasn't really doing this for the power. He really wanted to help them. These were people—*his* people. Perry had never really belonged to a group, being average and all. Sarah and James were great friends, but they weren't eagle Mews. These were eagles. Eagles that could talk and reason. They were like him. Talking with Bran and Dan all night long, learning about their childhood, had changed the way he saw them.

"I am ready for the trial," Perry said with a loud voice.

Beulah made a motion with his head that looked like a nod. "*Survive the trial and we shall serve you*," he said. "*Fail, and the death in the valley shall be your punishment.*"

The gathering, including Uncle Felix, chorused: *Survive the trial and we shall serve you. Fail, and the death in the valley shall be your punishment.*

"Thanks a lot for the vote of confidence," Perry muttered.

Uncle Felix poked him at the back. "Go ahead and change. They'll lead you to the trial grounds. It's somewhere north of here."

Perry gazed at his uncle for a long while, then grabbed him into a hug.

"It'll turn out fine," Uncle Felix said, patting him on the back.

Perry pulled away, turned to face the White Mountain on the horizon, and took off running.

"Good luck!" Uncle Felix's voice was drowned by the sound of hundred large eagles flapping their wings.

Within seconds, Perry had garnered enough speed to transform. He could feel his eagle pulse in every part of his body, ready to come forth. Yet, he kept running. First, because he wasn't eager to get to the trial. Second, because the last time he had transformed into the eagle, he had been stuck that way. Ice crunched under his feet. Icy, stingy air burned through his nostrils. When his chest began to hurt for the pounding of his heart, he knew it was time to change.

Perry shut his eyes, leaped off the ground, and burst into a massive eagle. His wings were stretched before they were fully wings. His tail was stretched as well. He soared less than two yards above the ground, creating a turbulence in his wake. He continued that way until the mountain got too close and he had to rise above it. When they were past the mountain, Perry was above the clouds and at the tip of the advancing company.

Bran and Dan had somehow managed to desert their positions in the company and flew side by side with him, Bran to his left and Dan to his right. Behind Perry, about twenty yards away, the five followed. Behind them still, a hundred birds filled the sky at different levels, their wings spread out to trap the cold winds. They looked like an army going to war.

No one spoke. Perry was left to his churning thoughts. The closer they got to the trial grounds, the more scared he became.

They flew for about thirty more minutes before the army fell behind, leaving the five, Perry, Bran, and Dan. Beulah didn't seem to mind.

"*So,*" Perry said to the two eagles beside him, "*your sister, Noniella. She didn't come to wave me goodbye?*" Perry didn't expect it, but when he said that, he felt a tiny bit of hurt.

"*Not everyone came out, Perry,*" Bran replied in his icy voice. The impudent tone was gone. They were now friends. Perry couldn't tell if it was because his uncle and Noniella had both told them to be nice to him or because they really liked him. He hoped it was the latter. "*Only the army came out.*"

That surprised Perry. "*Your army numbers in the hundreds? Are you saying there's hundreds of more eagles left in the mountain?*"

"*Yes,*" Bran said. "*That's excluding the soldiers that were left to guard our home.*"

"*No offense, guys,*" Perry said, "*but who are you guarding against? You guys live in the middle of nowhere.*"

"*Perry, evil is everywhere,*" Dan replied. "*We get attacked by evil nature just as much as you do. Hubats, Fargons, Kreckuns, and the lot of them.*" Then Dan's voice turned dark. "*Many have died because of these attacks, especially now that we don't have our powers. Our mother died in one of these attacks.*"

"*Noniella's mother and father died in one of these attacks, too,*" Bran added. "*Our father took her in as one of his own when this happened.*"

Perry could feel their hurt. He sighed and just kept flying. It was all he could do.

"*Guys,*" he said after some time, "*I'm going to give everything that I have to retrieve that flag, I promise you this. I'm not the smartest of Mews, nor have I been doing this for a long time. But I will try and try until I am dead or have returned with that flag.*" Perry didn't expect to feel good after saying something like that, but he did. He would give anything for his people. He knew they would do the same for him.

They soared for some time before they got to the valley. They descended and circled twice. They must have left the Arctic Circle because there was no ice around. The valley was large and tucked neatly between two green mountains. A thick blanket of fog covered the depression and hid whatever lay there in wait for him. At the south end of the valley, Perry could make out a doorway whose walls and lintel were the fog itself.

"This is where we leave you Perry, son of Johnson, heir of Pranis," Beulah said, matching Perry's vector. Bran and Dan had fallen back to allow their father talk to him.

"I must say, I misjudged you the first time you waltzed into our territory. But I have watched you, Perry. I have heard you talk. I have seen through your heart. You are a boy of strong courage. All I can say is good luck." Beulah fell away and flew back south. The remaining four followed suit.

Bran and Dan circled once more with him. *"When you retrieve the flag, we'll feel the power return to us and so will you. Head south and fly low. You won't miss the White Mountain,"* Dan said.

"Don't get iced down there," Bran said. *"If Pranis could do it, you can do it, too."*

"Thanks, guys. Now go before your father gets mad."

They fell away and were soon lost behind the horizon. The sun was already rising, laying light to everything except the valley. Perry circled again, trying to make out what was underneath the white mist. But, no matter the angle, the mist remained impenetrable to his eyes.

Perry descended to the earth and transformed, falling to his knees at the base of the mountain. The air smelled fresh with leaves. The ground was wet with dew. The shrubs and trees along the mountainside glittered with silvery water bubbles. Ahead, the wall of white mist rose several yards high and rolled over the valley. The doorway stood open at the bottom of the mountainside; all that proceeded from it was light.

Perry looked around. Not a sign of life. The place had a creepy feel to it, like people were watching him. He pushed himself up, scraping wet sand off his knees. As he approached the doorway, he noticed things to the left and right of the dirt path. It was as if a veil had been lifted from his eyes. There were tombstones sticking up from the grass. Two on his left, three on his right. On these tombstones, there were scribblings in English. He walked by, reading each word. *Mind. Will. Imagination. Thoughts. Emotions.*

Perry paused after the final tombstone and began to mule over the importance of these stones. He felt like he was in math class. He simply had no idea what they meant. Uncle Felix had said that there were five tests. There were five tombs here. It could mean that he might die in any of these tests. Maybe, it was a warning about the severity of the trial. *Anyone who isn't ready to face death, please go back.*

Perry approached the doorway. Now close to the light, he could see a door turned inwards. Both the doorway and the door were sculptured out of white stone. On the door was written: *Can You School Your Mind?*

Yes, Perry thought and walked into the light.

22
FIVE TESTS
MAKE A TRIAL

P erry felt a warm tingle which lasted for three seconds. As soon as it was gone, he saw himself hanging by an invisible thread high up his high school's basketball arena.

Panic struck Perry with intense immediacy.

Pain. He felt pain. His vision blurred, bloodied.

He was Eagle. He was human.

Everything was just so confusing. He was delirious. How had he gotten up here? He felt as if his flesh was being ripped apart piece by bloody piece. There was a taunting laughter. He felt as if his feathers were being torn out of his flesh, slowly, in ways that ensured maximum pain.

Perry screamed. His eagle whistled. Yet, there was no respite. In fact, his scream seemed to encourage his torturer. Perry craned his neck to look around. Pain shot up his head in hot flashes. When had he been in a car wreck? He couldn't make out anything in the red smear. But below, he saw shapes moving. Creatures that went on all fours, about ten or twelve of them, moving like crocodiles beneath him; waiting for him to fall.

These creatures howled like wolves yet roared like lions.

Another piece of his flesh ripped. Another feather yanked out. Another shrill scream escaped his mouth. Another unbearable jolt of pain. Perry squeezed his eyes shut and wished it would all just go away, and for a second it did. But, it was just a moment. Because it came back with force.

Perry screamed again. His sweatshirt had been ripped off his body and fell to pieces on the floor. Claw marks stretching his small chest. The marks were about five inches long and maybe two apart, three of them.

Perry concentrated on transforming. He couldn't. Something was blocking his eagle. Perry glanced at his stretched arms. They were covered in blood, but no piece seemed to be missing. His confusion rose. He felt so much pain and there was so much blood, yet, there was no injury. Perry thought back to the...

He screamed again. His head swayed as he hovered on the brink, about to fall into the clutches of death. There might not be an injury, but death was as good as death. *Can you school your mind*, the inscription on the door had read.

Perry shut his eyes and wished for the pains to vanish. They did. It was like shutting a door when a horde of people was trying to get in. Perry's torturer resisted him. And every time Perry faltered, the pain came back with rabid intensity. It seemed like his mind was more inclined to helping his three-clawed torturer than fighting for Perry. Perry had to discipline his mind to obey him; it was his after all.

Even as the battle in his mind raged, Perry could feel his life slipping away. He was dripping blood even though there was no opening in his body. He was weakening even though there was no reason why he should. He then realized that it was all in his mind. But just because it was in his mind did not make it less real.

Perry mustered his last strength and forced the vicious image out of his mind. Something somewhere snapped, and Perry fell to the floor. His journey to the hard ground lasted three seconds. The impact should have killed him, but it didn't. Neither did it maim him. Why should it, when the twelve horrendous beasts rushing towards him could?

Perry couldn't tell if they were wolves or tigers. Just that they were furry and had big acid-wet canines and glowing eyes. A wave of nausea sent bile to his lips and when he opened his mouth, a strong roar exactly like a lion's burst forth. Perry shot to his feet and grabbed the first beast out of its lunge. Using his bare hands, he tore it apart.

This is all in my mind, Perry thought, slaying the beasts one after the other. In his mind, he made the rules. The last beast was bigger, but he tore it apart all the same, though it took some exertion from him. This exertion manifested as another earsplitting roar.

Perry was on his knees amidst a pile of ripped wolves, his chest heaving and his body bare, when a door ahead opened. He had passed the first test.

Perry stood and went to the door. Light was all he could see—light that blinded him. The door, as it was in the beginning, was turned inwards. Inscribed on the door was: *How Strong Is Your Will?*

Perry walked through.

After three seconds of a warm tingly sensation, he found himself in the stands of a soccer pitch. He was in the southern end. All the way across to the northern end, there was an open door. All he had to do was make his way across the field, and then he was on to the third test. The only problem was the hundreds of Hubats perched along the stands on the west and east of the field.

Perry tried summoning the eagle. It was still being suppressed because it wouldn't budge. He found an access way to the tracks and then crossed onto the field. The moment he set foot on the grass, the Hubats stirred. Perry took off, making a beeline for the door. These Hubats were smaller than the ones he had seen in Brooklyn. At the center of the pitch, they met.

They slammed into him like tiny projectiles at full speed. Perry kept running. Fangs sank into his neck, chest, and legs. Perry kept running. There was darkness around him. The Hubats swarmed him, scratching his face and exposed skin. Perry's heart began to thump. He could barely see where he was heading and the impacting Hubats were constantly jeering him off course. The bites became more painful and constant.

Perry was forced to slow down and use his hands to lead the way. He shut his eyes. One Hubat bit into his left calf. Perry stumbled, slapped the creature off his legs, rose again, and kept trudging forward. The swarm buzzed incessantly in his ears. That's why Perry didn't hear the creature bound for him. By the time he felt its presence, it was already too late.

The creature's hands or paws or palms—whatever had hit him—were soft, but the impact knocked Perry into the air. Perry came to his senses back at the southern end. He laid on the tracks gasping for breath. His body was on fire. Perry moaned softly, craning his neck to look back at the field. The Hubat formed a black buzzing mist at the center and much of the northern side of the pitch. Somewhere in that mist, he saw a white-furred beast roam.

Perry saw no way he could make it past the swarm without his eagle. Aside from being immune to high falls, he had no special power and those creatures were "special" creatures. It was just so frustrating.

Perry sat up gently. He didn't want to move his body too much since they still burned with pain. He looked at his leg. Four holes formed a reddish circle where the Hubat had bit him. Somewhere off to his right, away from the Hubats, Perry's eyes caught a sign that read: WAY OUT OF HERE. There was an arrow that pointed up. That was when Perry looked up for the first time. White Mist. But where the arrow pointed, sunlight penetrated. He could go over there and fly away. He didn't have to suffer like this.

It could end now. No need to die.

Perry jumped onto the pitch and ran.

Yes, he could end it now and go, but he would be condemning his parents to death. He would be breaking a promise to his friends, Bran and Dan. Perry plunged into the dark mist. He blocked the pain out of his mind. He refused to regard the fangs sinking into parts of his body, nor did he bother about the annoying buzz. He was madly slapping the air around him, his ears alert.

Perry felt a rumble begin in the pit of his stomach. By the time it had worked its way to his chest it had transformed into an urge to vomit. When it finally came out, it was a roar. Then, Perry felt a surge of strength. He felt the rush of air that heralded a swinging paw. Then, Perry bent on all fours and leaped into the air, the whole stunt taking him a second to perform. He was airborne for a short time. He landed and skidded to a halt off the field and onto the tracks of the northern side.

Perry fell to his knees first and breathed through his mouth. He wasn't sure what had happened back there. When he felt he could continue, he rose up and slugged to the door. Inscribed on the door was: *Your Imagination. Your Reality...*

Perry sluggard on in.

He was in a large white room. That was all. No creature, no monster, no features, just an open door full of light over on the other side. Perry judged the distance to the door to be half a block or less. He started the walk and saw himself walking along Third Avenue. The door stood open exactly half a block away, but it was just like the real Third Avenue: the skyscrapers, the fast pedestrian traffic, the honks, and all.

Perry remembered that the last time he was on Third Avenue, Sarah and James were with him. Instantly, Sarah and James popped up beside him, walking with him. They didn't look at Perry; they only looked straight on and kept walking. When he stopped, they stopped. When he walked, they walked. They neither spoke nor asked questions.

Perry began to understand what the room he stepped into was supposed to do. What it was supposed to *test*, he didn't yet know. But the possibility of having your every thought actualized was as exciting as it was daunting. What if he thought about all the scary stuff he had heard about the sea monster? It didn't bode well with Perry. He picked up pace towards the door. His last brush with the creature was at that private dock, what if the sea monster had sprung a second earlier? What if Perry had flown a second later? Reacted a second later?

Suddenly, Perry found himself in that same spot on the dock. A green mist blurred beneath the surface of the river to his left. Sarah and James floated away—Perry became terrified. He saw the door ahead, but abandoned it, choosing rather to put as much space between him and the monster as possible. The sea monster broke through the plywood in front of Perry and towered high. It was covered head to bottom by a cyclone of water.

Perry's first thought was to turn and run. But then, where would he run to? He was still in the imagination room, so he didn't need to fight. Perry imagined an army of Fire Breathers led by Pranis charging the sea monster.

Immediately, there was a loud eagle whistle behind him.

Before Perry could turn, a silver Mew eagle shot past him and engaged the sea monster. Behind him was a host of Mew-large eagles who attacked the sea monster as well. While the sea monster was distracted, Perry sneaked by and slipped into the light. The door had said: *Mind Your Thoughts.*

He was on a path through a thick forest. It was evening. He had a shield in his hands. In the distance, he could see the door and its light. He started along the path, thinking about how miserable his life was. Perry heard a silent whirr. He had his shield up in time to block the long fiery arrow. The thing disappeared on impact.

He stopped in his tracks, the shield still raised. His heart was racing. *What happened?* he wondered.

Perry started along the path again, thinking about how his mother had abandoned him, and sent him off to the Arctic Circle. A whirr. The shield came up. The first arrow struck the shield, the second struck his waist. His knees buckled under his weight. The shield fell to the ground, though he still hung on to it.

Perry looked at his waist. The arrow was gone, leaving behind a painful wound and a surge of bad thoughts towards his mother. Perry held his mind at bay, realizing what this room was all about. Evil thoughts were fiery arrows. If he could not think any evil thought for a few moments, he could make it out of here alive.

Perry struggled to his feet and limped on.

The bad thoughts came bursting forth into his mind. Perry went on his knees and shoved his shield into the ground. He opposed the bad thoughts with good ones. Mother loved him. Mother sent him here because she wanted to protect him. Yes, he was average before, but being here, trying to help the Fire Breathers was extraordinary. The fiery darts came at him from every direction, but they were deflected by a blue shimmering shield that had formed around him.

Perry kept the goods thoughts flowing. He stood up and limped on, thinking only good.

When he came to the fifth door, the fiery darts of evil ceased. The shield, having no more usefulness, vanished. He read the inscription on the door: *Control Your Emotions.*

Perry walked through.

He was back at his parents' apartment building. He stood across the street from the building gazing up at the apartment. The windows were boarded up as he remembered. It was late afternoon, and no one paid him any attention. Perry wondered what he was doing here when a scream pierced the air.

It was Lisa. It was coming from their apartment. Without thinking, Perry leaped into the road. Car screeches rent the air. Perry was across and racing up the stairs. Lisa screamed again, this one more guttural. Perry's heart was pounding and his head throbbing when he got to the door. He didn't knock. He broke down the door.

In the dining room, a huge figure held Lisa against the wall by her throat. Lisa's eyes were glazed over. The gurgles seized with a final wisp of breath. Perry saw that he had come too late. He came just in time to see the last thread of life leave his sister.

The man, not satisfied by her death, snapped her neck for good measure and threw her body away like it were a ragged doll.

Perry was struck with a fit of red-hot madness.

He hollered like a barbarian and lunged for the man. The man was three times Perry's size with rippling biceps. Yet, Perry overpowered him and bashed his fists into the man's face over, and over, and over again. With each swing, his mind replayed his sister's death, and he hit harder. His hands came off with blood, but he did not relent. His hands came off transformed with claws and fur, but he would not relent. His hands came off with ripped tissues, but he hit harder.

He wept and bashed the man's head again and again.

The man laid there, unconscious, ready to die at one more blow. Perry raised his hands, his heart swelling with grief and his mind beclouded by fury. He then saw that with each strike, he was becoming the very evil he was fighting against. Furs had sprung on his body. Two horns on his head. A tail from his buttocks. It was the perfect picture of evil; *the* evil—*d*evil.

Perry dropped his hands, letting go of his fury.

The image vanished, and he was back within the white mist in the valley. Ahead, he saw the doorway. Through the doorway, he saw the green mountainside.

Perry dragged himself to his feet. He passed through the fifth doorway into the open air. The sun was at its peak, the air dry and crisp. Perry took in a deep breath, letting it out slowly. His hands trembled. He had not yet recovered from his sister's faked death. He may never.

Perry walked over to the flag which hung by a squat pole rooted in the ground. It was a simple red flag. The only thing that marked it as the

Fire Breather's property was the golden weave of an eagle's head in the center. When he touched it, two things happened. One, it came free from the pole. Two, he felt his eagle break free of its suppression. Nothing spectacular happened after this, but Perry could feel it in him that he had gotten the Fire Breathers' abilities.

Perry looked around the foot of the mountain for nothing in particular. He thought he would be excited about surviving the trial, but he wasn't. In fact, he felt sad. Perry knew he shouldn't be. His sister hadn't really died, had she? She was still safe in Nevada with Jane who was a huge buzzard, wasn't she? But, did Perry know this for sure? If the Crofts had gone for his parents, attacked him and Jake at their house, what's to stop them from attacking Lisa and Jane at their cliff house in Nevada?

Perry pushed these thoughts to the back of his mind. One thing was clear though. He was leaving for Manhattan at dawn tomorrow. Perry walked some way up the mountain, wrapping the flag around his body. He turned and ran down the mountain. Near the base, he leaped into the air and transformed with a flash of light.

He climbed the air and soared towards the White Mountain. Towards home.

23
PERRY FLIES BACK TO NEW YORK

Perry got back to the Arctic Circle in the evening. When he got close to the mountain, Bran and Dan joined him. They were different: their chests looked like gleeds, their wings were made of sharp metals, and thus glinted in the setting sun. They did not speak. It was as if they could perceive his depression. Soon, others joined them and they became a company of metal winged eagles. Even Yates was among the birds that escorted him back to the mountain.

The expression each bird had on its face was similar. Their eyes burned with concentration. Their faces tightened with a frown. It wasn't a mistake that he was at the center of the moving army. It was a statement, a promise. He had fought for them. He had risked his life to help them. Now, they would fight for him in turn. They would give their lives for him. They would serve him.

As the White Mountain loomed into view, the birds began to whistle. It was a sonorous soothing sound and went like a wave. It started from one part under heaven, swept across the skies, and ended in the other part. Soon, they began to get responses from the mountain. Whistles of joy. But it wasn't joy that Perry had retrieved the flag; they knew that the moment he touched it back at the valley of death. It was joy that he had returned—their savior. Instead of heading into the mountain, they led him away towards the van. Many more eagles joined them, all massive like him, all having chests like glowing coal.

Once at the van, the eagles dispersed from him. Only Bran and Dan remained. It was as if they had read Perry's mind, because he didn't want them gone. Strangely, he wanted them at his side.

Beneath, he could see that a lot of birds, including the five, had assembled before the minivan. Perry broke speed and shot towards the ground. He stretched his claws forward like he was about to catch prey, then transformed. His feet touched the ground and he was walking. Bran and Dan perched on the minivan.

It was one of the very few times he had transformed seamlessly. He should be excited, but he wasn't. Not after what had happened in that last test.

Perry approached the five, folded the red flag, and placed it before them. "Here's your flag," he muttered.

The five bowed their beaks. The host of eagles perched on the floor behind them bowed as well. Perry noticed that dotting the area around the minivan, sticks had been arranged like a bonfire without the fire.

"We are forever indebted to you Perry, son of Johnson, heir of Pranis," Beulah said in a humble voice. Then, he bent his head backwards and his burning chest intensified: fire gushed out of his mouth in a sustained flow. The remaining four, as well as the hundreds of birds on the ground, did the same. Pillars of fire filled the air.

Uncle Felix who had been standing at the side all along came over to Perry and whispered, "It's a tradition to celebrate victory. You are now considered the leader of the Fire Breathers. You did it, Perry."

The birds turned their beaks to the sticks. Smoke pillared to the clouds. Instantly, Perry was enraptured in a blanket of warmth. Though the smell of burning wood sickened him, he didn't complain.

The singing and dancing began. The birds clapped their wings and danced around the fires whistling softly and creating a swinging melody that soothed Perry's soul. There was a log of wood beside the door. Perry sat down there and watched the celebration, not wanting to take part in it any further.

Uncle Felix went inside the minivan for a moment. He returned with a blanket which Perry wrapped around his bare body and a mug of steaming hot chocolate. Perry thanked him, sipping, and watching the birds dance.

Uncle Felix sat down next to him. "Perry, what you have done today, many eagle Mews have died trying to do. Your parents would be as proud of you as I am." He was beaming,

"You knew the trial would be easy, didn't you?"

Uncle Felix considered his question for a second. "Perry, that trial is anything but easy. What you did, not many could have done. Remember what I told you about the tests? Each test was designed to test you as a person, Perry. You are young and without scruples. You've barely faced the world." Then he sighed. "Age is the real evil, Perry. If you had taken these tests ten years from now, we might be hearing a different story."

Perry's body still hurt from the trial, but he didn't seem to be injured. All the scars had somehow vanished the moment he stepped beyond the mist.

"Uncle Felix," Perry said, "I saw Lisa in the final test."

"You did?" he replied with a sudden interest and a twinge of fear. "Tell me."

Perry told him everything. From the time he was outside the apartment to the time he almost killed the huge man. He told Uncle Felix how Lisa had died and how he had felt—how he *still* felt. Uncle Felix kept his face straight throughout the whole narration. But Perry sensed people's emotions well, and he could sense that Uncle Felix was agitated.

"Perry, there's something about the trial I think you should know," he began. "The trial is the handwork of the evil. It's a way to prevent the Fire Breathers from rising to their true potentials. I'm afraid, Perry, that the moment you walked into that mist, you surrendered yourself to the evil and so it searched you. It knows your fears, Perry. It knows your sister is your weakest link—your Achilles' heel." He paused as he always did when he considered whether Perry was old enough to know the next thing he was about to say. "You've grown stronger today, Perry. You've become a real threat. The evil, or what you call evil nature, will strike at your heart to weaken you."

That got Perry's attention. He was standing and speaking in a loud voice. "Are you saying Lisa's life is actually in danger?" Perry didn't even wait for him to answer. He was walking away from the party into the darkness beyond, where he planned to transform and take off for their cliff house. He heard Uncle Felix run after him and two birds hover along.

"Perry!" Uncle Felix called once they were beyond the fire. "Perry, wait!"

Perry stopped short, his eagle already filling his body. "What, Uncle?!" he shot back, angry.

"Where are you going to?"

Perry growled. "To warn Jane. To save Lisa."

"You can't do that, Perry." He was gasping.

"Why can't I?" Perry's head was buzzing. He had summoned the eagle; now, he was having a hard time keeping it summoned and not transforming.

"Because you have to kill the sea monster."

"Why does it have to be me?" Perry croaked. "I have control of the Fire Breathers. Take control of the lot of them and go after the sea monster. I'm going to keep my sister safe."

Perry turned to go, but Uncle Felix held him back.

His eyes softened. "Perry, not much is known about the sea monster. But, what I do know is that only an eagle *Mew* can kill the beast because the beast came forth from the eagle. As you may have figured out already, the beast is your challenge. It's your exam. No one is going to take it for you."

Perry tried to go but Uncle Felix held him still. "Now you can walk away and go warn your sister. But you'll be condemning your mother and father to death. And should Joanna's blood spill in that sea four days from now, the sea monster will become indestructible. Let me go warn your sister. Where is she?"

"With Jane at our cliff house in Nevada."

"Good. I'll go and warn them. You go after the sea monster."

Perry considered it and decided it was his best option. After all, Lisa needed their parents alive. Perhaps, Jane could keep Lisa safe till Uncle Felix got there. Perry followed Uncle Felix back to the minivan where they were met by Yates.

"*Perry,*" Yates called in reverence, "*I have the whole army waiting to leave at first light tomorrow. We'll follow you into battle against the sea monster.*" He said this with great boldness and pride, like it was an honorable thing to follow Perry into battle.

"No, Yates," Perry replied, catching Uncle Felix off guard.

"Perry—"

"These people need protection, Uncle," Perry said. "I can't take away the only protection they have. The army stays here."

"At least take a few," Uncle Felix pressed. "Take Bran and Dan."

"*Yes, take us,*" Bran pleaded. "*We can get you to the sky city in three days.*"

"All right," Perry conceded. He had grown to like the two birds. They called New York sky city because of the tall buildings.

"Yates," Perry addressed the eagle in his most serious voice. "Tomorrow, I'll leave before dawn with Bran and Dan. I want you and eight of your best to accompany the phoenix to Nevada to warn my sister of an impending attack. The remaining army should stay here and protect the pack."

Uncle Felix agreed with Perry's wisdom, nodding thoughtfully.

"*Agreed,*" Yates replied. He turned and flew away.

After watching the eagles for a while longer, Perry rose and ambled to the door of the minivan. Uncle Felix suggested they join the celebration, but Perry was in no mood for celebration. All he thought about was his sister's safety. Perry changed into the night robes that had been laid out for him by the phoenix and pulled the bed sheets around him.

Perry thought sleep would come easily since he was exhausted. But he was wrong. He lay in bed replaying Lisa's death in his mind. When he finally fell asleep, the singing and flapping outside had ceased, the popping fire had fallen silent, and the world had descended back into a state of tranquility.

♦ ♦ ♦

Perry woke at least an hour before dawn. Uncle Felix was already awake and about somewhere outside. Perry brushed his teeth, washed his face, and changed into the new clothes that Uncle Felix had picked out for him; a red shirt and jeans. These were the same color of clothes he had worn on the day of the Fall Ritual. It only seemed fitting. With it, he had begun all this. With it, he would end it.

Perry went outside. Bran and Dan were waiting for him, alert and ready to go, as well as Uncle Felix, Beulah, and Yates. Up in the clouds, as many as nine eagles circled the area.

"They've been circling the minivan all night," Uncle Felix said. He stood beside the log of a tree in front of the minivan where Beulah and Yates were perched.

Perry gave him a curious glance.

"Your protection detail," Uncle Felix explained with a bit of a chuckle. "Beulah is here to convince you that it is reckless to take only two eagles back to Manhattan. He says even though he lives to serve you, he suggests you take at least four squadrons with you."

"Can he not speak for himself?" Perry commented. Before any reply could be made, he continued. "Look, I appreciate the offer, but the eagles best remain here. People are afraid of me as it is. If they knew I had in my control an army of fire-breathing, metal winged, Mew-massive eagles, they'd go crazy."

Uncle Felix seemed amazed at his reply.

"Thanks for everything," Perry said in parting. "I have to go now."

Perry broke off into a run. He was rising into the air seconds later, his wings stretched to their lengths. Bran and Dan formed around him along with the nine already circling.

"*They'll follow us to the edge of the Arctic Circle before returning,*" Bran said.

Perry bobbed his beak once to show he understood.

The White Mountain and the minivan quickly fell below the horizon as the group sped south. They flew nonstop until they got to Victoria Island. There they circled twice, saying their goodbyes to the nine eagles that had escorted them. Then they parted ways. At the suggestion of Bran, Perry and the two brothers climbed several thousand feet until they were beyond the clouds before they continued south. That way, Bran told him, they were covering more distance even if they were going at a slower speed, which they weren't. They landed only twice. On the first day, they landed in Yellowknife, Canada. On the second day, they landed in Ontario, Canada, where a nice old lady was kind enough to give him some food. While Perry ate, the two brothers hunted.

The sun was already pulling its rays down the horizon when they entered New York. They flew too high to be noticed by any searching Mew or sentry. They didn't descend until it was almost dark and they were near Perry's apartment building. Bran remained outside looking for signs of trouble while Dan and Perry flew into the apartment through an open window. They had to tear through the police tape.

They found the house turned upside down.

Dan flew on into the other rooms ahead of him while Perry transformed back. He remained in his room, looking around. His drawers had been upended, his bed ripped to shreds. The light fixture above had been shattered. What had happened here? Perry recalled when he had escaped. Jake had been trapped in here so Perry could make it out. Perry had been so engrossed in his problems that he hadn't thought of Jake since then. He wondered what had happened to his brother.

In the dining room, there was nothing much to see. The place had been torn apart. The table was broken, the TV probably stolen because it no longer hung on the wall. The room was dark and stuffy. The door to the apartment was sealed off by police tape. Perry headed in that direction.

"Come on, Dan," he said, bending through the yellow tape. "There's nothing here."

Perry went to the roof next. He remembered dropping his bag there before he had taken off. He found the bag sitting on the gravel, untouched. Bran joined them. Perry searched through the bag and found his phone. Sarah had left him several messages. He played through every one of them. Sarah had worried and cried and grieved over him. The last message included a desperate invitation to her house. She had heard that their apartment had been ransacked and that he no longer had a place to stay. Her parents were not in town and no one had seen her elder brothers Don and Chase in days. Could he come and sleep over? At least until the crisis cleared.

"*That sounds like a good idea, boss,*" Bran said.

Perry was mildly shocked at first when he heard Bran's comment. He had forgotten that he had two formidable eagles hovering above him.

"Yeah?"

"*Yes, boss,*" Dan said. "*It's too dangerous to remain here.*"

"Okay." Perry rose to his feet. "Let's go." He tucked the phone into his pocket and ran for the edge of the building. They flew for seven minutes before they were circling Sarah's parents' house. The light in Sarah's room was on. Once Bran signaled that it was okay, Perry whistled.

He heard running footsteps. Bran and Dan ducked behind the building. Sarah stuck her head out her window and looked up. She was wearing a white vest and her faded pink pajamas. When she saw Perry, she beamed and waved for him to come in. He swung into her room and landed as Perry, the human, again.

Sarah jumped into him. She was sobbing. "Thank God you're alive. We thought you were dead." Then she pushed him away and frowned. "You *are* alive. Where were you? Why didn't you return our calls?"

Perry smiled. "It's a long story. One that I'll tell some other time. But now, we have to help my parents."

Sarah's face turned dark. "Oh my gosh, Perr. I'm sorry. It's horrible what my brothers are doing to your parents and Richard. My mother won't let me anywhere near them. How are we going to save your parents?"

Perry smiled. He never thought he would feel this elated to say this. "We are going to kill the sea monster."

Sarah looked at him for a slight moment with an eye of wonder. "You look different, Perr. You look...more powerful."

"I'm hungry, though," Perry said, and the two eagles burst into the room.

Sarah's reaction was immediate. She backpedaled, releasing a sharp, short scream.

"It's okay," Perry muttered, holding out a hand to her. "They're here to help."

"Are they Mews?" Sarah asked, taking his hand but remaining frightened.

"They might be as big as us Mews, but they're not Mews. They are—"

"The Fire Breathers of the north," Sarah said, wonder lighting her eyes. She looked at him. "That's where you went to, isn't it?"

Perry didn't reply. But, that didn't stop her from drawing conclusions.

"You took the trial...and won. That's why they followed you here. You command nature's greatest aerial army, don't you? You're master of the Fire Breathers." She said that with awe.

"Sarah?"

"Huh?"

"Food?"

"Oh." Sarah left the room. However, Perry knew he would still have to confirm all her conclusions. It was nearly impossible to fool a brilliant girl when all the evidence she needed was in her room. Dan and Bran stayed near the window, vigilant as always. Perry heard Sarah convince her aunt that she thought she had seen a mouse scurry in her room and that was why she had screamed. She spent a few more minutes assuring her that everything was fine now and that she just wanted some food.

She came back to the room with a sack of his favorite fries and a cup of orange juice. Perry ate while Sarah admired the creatures in the corner near the window.

Perry felt it from Bran before he spoke.

"*Boss,*" Bran said, "*there's a falcon three minutes away coming in from the east. It seems to be headed here.*"

Perry glanced at Sarah, who couldn't hear the Fire Breather. "Bran tells me there's a falcon approaching."

"It's James," she said. "I sent him a text message."

Perry was done with his food when James came into the room. They embraced each other.

"I'm sorry about your parents, Perry," James said, now sober. "My father wanted to lead the elite Mew against the sentence, but your father told him not to. There had already been a rebellion. There was no need for another."

"Where are your parents now?" Perry asked.

"Dunno," the boy said. "They got summoned to Denver early this morning. They've not returned or called." James glanced at the eagles. "Fire Breathers," he noted. "You retrieved the flag, I see."

Perry sat on the rug and motioned for them to do the same. "This stays within our group. Is that clear? No one can know that I command the Fire Breathers. At least not yet."

Sarah shook her head in that could-you-be-any-more-daft sort of way. "Really, Perr? No one's gonna put you in danger among us."

"Sarah tells me we're going after the sea monster tomorrow?" James said next. There was an excitement in his voice and in his eyes.

Perry nodded and told them his plan. After they had fine-tuned the plan, they packed their tired selves onto Sarah's bed and fell asleep, Bran and Dan keeping watch at the window.

24
ATTACK OF THE SEA MONSTER

The birds came in low and hard, flying in an arrow formation. Perry's brown golden eagle at the tip, Sarah's white owl to his left, and James's black falcon to his right. It was almost midday and they were going to crash a sacrifice.

They had gotten ready just before dawn. They didn't have to because they were slated to leave by ten since the sacrifice was at twelve. But, not one of them could sleep much knowing that they were planning on killing the sea monster today. So, on edge, they waited until it was time to go to animal control.

This part of the plan was to cause enough nuisance so that the cops and animal control would be dispatched, and then the two eagles would lead them to the dock. They had been successful. About three minutes ago, Perry, James, and Sarah had parted ways with Dan and Bran. Now, they only had less than thirty minutes before the two Fire Breathers led the police to the dock. Should they defeat the sea monster and the Mews present decided they still wanted to kill him or his parents, the police would be there to protect them.

Perry saw the platform before the others did. In the distance, thousands of feet below, there was a small wooden platform lining the dock. His mother, father, and Richard were on their knees, bound by ropes. Don and Chase stood on the platform addressing a small crowd of about fifty Mews standing around. Nearer to the platform, Perry saw four elite Mews. He was a little surprised by the elite Mew presence since the Fortins were their leaders. So, he asked James about it.

"*They're undercover, sort of,*" James replied. "*My father left them instructions to stop the sacrifice before anyone gets killed and get your family out of there. They were instructed to act as though it was their initiative so my father would be distanced from the act. That way, it wouldn't be a rebellion but a crime. One that would save your family.*"

Perry nodded.

They were still flying over houses, but they were closing in on the sea. Once they were close enough, a huge storm erupted from the sea at the edge of the horizon. A massive cylinder of constantly rotating water shot to a height of about a hundred yards, moving towards the dock. Within the huge wall of water, Perry saw hundreds of Hubats flying around, their cries and shrieks reaching him. Beyond the black mist, he saw the sea monster. His heart jerked up to his beak.

Thoughts of saving his parents and running away crossed his mind.

Tiny figures way down at the platform scurried around. Some of the Mews were running away from the water. Others stood, though keeping a safe distance between themselves and the platform. The elite Mews stood their ground, their eyes darting between the approaching wave of destruction and the Crofts. Don and Chase were in awe, but they didn't seem frightened.

Don pulled out a dagger, faced the rolling wave, and yelled his obeisance to the creature. Then he turned and said. "Accept their blood."

Perry whistled. The sound reverberated across the dock like thunder.

All heads turned to the skies.

Perry descended like lightning. Don pulled out a small black pistol from his back. Perry didn't have enough time to dodge it; he was coming in too hot. Mother screamed. Perry pushed his claws forward to cut down his speed and pulled his wings around his chest to form a shield. His wings turned to metal blades.

Perry heard the roar of the pistol. He felt the bullet deflect off his wings, doing no harm. Perry spread out his wings with force, catching Don's face in the arc. Don spun into the air and fell to the ground, dazed. The elite Mews jumped into action. One seized Chase, who was still stunned by his appearance, while the others set his family free.

Perry transformed and landed softly on the ground. He pointed his hands at the Mews gazing at him. "You can either stay here and die," he yelled, "or you can run for your lives!"

He didn't need to say anymore. They all took off like a pack of scared dogs. It wasn't so much because of the sea monster as it was because of what they had seen him do; deflect a bullet with his wings.

"Perry!" A hand grabbed him and squeezed. It was his mother. Father and Richard hugged him in turn. They looked worn out and tired. They had bruises and smudges all over their faces, and they smelt of salt water; otherwise, they seemed to be all right. Sarah and James came over to his side. Three of the elites gathered around.

"So, what next?" Father asked him.

Perry was a little surprised at this question. He thought he hadn't heard him well, so he looked around and saw that he had heard his father right! They were all staring at him. They were waiting for his instructions. They wanted to follow him into battle.

Perry nodded. He turned around. The storm was already upon them. He could feel millions of tiny water particles bash into his face at this coming of death.

"We kill the thing," Perry replied, lost for a moment in the swirling storm. He jumped off the ledge and was airborne again, climbing towards the sea monster. He felt no fear. He felt much anxiety. But one thing was certain; he would kill the sea monster.

The seconds trickled down, slow, as they neared the wall of water. The shrill sounds intensified. They began to hear deep moans from the green creature shielded by the water and Hubats.

"*Perry,*" his father said in his head, "*we'll pair up. I with James. Your mother with Sarah. Richard with Dean. Josh with Peter. We'll clear a path for you through the Hubats.*"

"Okay," Perry replied, assuming that the three elites with them were Dean, Josh, and Peter. He communicated this to Sarah and James while James communicated this to the elites. They paired up forming a kind of loose hedge around him.

Silence.

The wall of water hit them with a slap. They were through the wall a moment after they made contact. The Hubats rushed them like a swarm of bees. The Mews fought back with deadly precision. Sarah and mother, the two great white owls, were vicious killers—tearing Hubats apart with beaks and claws. James's falcon and Father's harrier were more efficient killers, picking the Hubats out of their kamikaze dives one after the other, never spending more than a second with one. The Hubats fell every moment, but that didn't diminish their numbers.

The group's advance had stopped as the horde of dark bat-like creatures thickened. Perry shot right past his coverage. His flight through the White Mountain helped him a little as he ducked every surge and struck when he couldn't dodge. But, they were just too much. Pieces of his feathers began to fall off his body as the black claws found home, leaving stings of pain behind.

At one point, Perry was subdued and submerged. They concentrated on his head, forcing him downwards. They wanted to drown him. Perry rounded his body with his wings. He let them push him to the water. Just as he was about to hit the surface of the water, his wings shot out as metal blades, shearing seven Hubats. His chest burned. He drew back his head and unleashed a flood of fire. He sustained the blast and shot back into the air. Hubats burned by the tens, the fire spreading by contact. Perry forced his way past the last wave of Hubats, leaving a trail of fire in his wake. At that moment, Perry came face to face with the sea monster.

It was green. It was big. It was like a giant serpent with two legs at its tail end, which were hidden by the water beneath. It had bony spines all along its muscled body. At its top there were two eyes, an open maw, and sharp fangs. The eyes seemed to look up instead of forward. Also, it had huge hands.

Perry ravaged its body with fire.

The hands tried to catch him, to swat him or squash him, but Perry was bullet fast and the hands were just too sluggish; snail slow. This continued for a while before Perry realized that he was doing as much damage as a fly on a human body. The only way to defeat the monster was to cut out its eye. But Perry had noticed that whenever he neared the eye, he felt a pull towards the creature. When he felt the pull, he slowly lost his will. His power. He knew if he looked into those eyes, it would be over.

How could he cut out the eyes without looking at it? As Perry ran the length of the creature, burning it with floods of fire from his mouth, an idea struck him. It was the only way he could see ending the battle. Yet, it was dangerous.

Perry flapped his wings and climbed the air. He passed the head of the creature, passed the weak swat of the creature, until he got to the ceiling of the wall of water. Then, he swooped around and transformed, falling as human towards the creature, his eyes clamped shut.

Perry's heart pounded.

Perry fell, his ears straining to measure distance, his senses on red alert. The monster moaned and wailed all in a bid to get his attention and to get him to open his eyes. Perry remained obstinate. The desire was strong to take one peek at the eyes of the creature, but he fought it. When he got to the right height, he tried to transform. It failed.

Perry panicked and opened his eyes. Black beady eyes met his, and just before he lost all will, he saw the creature smile as if saying: *got you*. He couldn't resist. He couldn't fight. He just fell, powerless.

For a moment, Perry was sure it was over as he fell to his death.

Then, like a surge, Perry's eagle forced its way to the surface, not to take over again this time, but to give him charge. Perry transformed with a blinding flash. The creature blinked for a moment. That short moment was all Perry needed for the connection to be broken. A flood of fire shot out of his beak and bashed into the creature's face just as it opened its eyes.

The sea monster wailed: a deep, slow rumble. It wriggled and began to go under water. Its eyes were charred. Perry shot after it, threw his claws into the eye sockets, and dug deep. The creature let loose another earth trembling wail. The Hubats howled shrilly in response, then converged on him. Before the first could get to him, Perry flapped once, and yanked out the two charred eyeballs from the creature's eye sockets.

The creature wailed. It wriggled like a giant earthworm in intense pain. Only, in this case, it was shrinking. Then, it was buried by the water. Perry squeezed his claws, turning the crisp eyeballs into dust.

The wall of water fell back to the ocean with a mighty splash.

It was all over.

Some Hubats fled when they saw that the sea monster had fallen. Other remained to fight. Whatever Hubats remained, Perry and his team annihilated them. When they were done cleaning up the last of the evil creatures, they cheered and chattered all the way back to the dock. The sea monster was dead. All was well.

Back at the dock, they were met by Louis and Daphne. The terrified expression on their faces told Perry that something was terribly wrong.

25

LISA

I t was Lisa, the Fortins had said.

Lisa.

The clouds streaked past him in a white blur. He was moving so fast that he could feel the turbulence he was creating in the wake of his tail. Bran and Dan were trying to keep up with him. They might have been Mew-large, but they weren't Mews, so they were not as fast as he was. They had cautioned him about his speed. He could shatter his bones, they had said.

Yes, he ran the risk of crushing himself at this terrifying speed. Yet, he didn't care. Lisa's life was in danger. A chill swept the edges of his wings. Perry pushed harder, tearing the air left and right with his beak. He was already feeling a strain in his bones.

The summons was fake, the Fortins had said. They had been jumped by the two living Red Tails and a pack of twelve low-life Mew scums. Daphne had scoffed. "They should have brought more," she had said. One of the attackers pled for mercy, confessing to them that Lisa had been captured and was being held captive at an address in Denver, Colorado. Once Perry had the address memorized, he had turned to go without uttering a word to anyone.

"Perry!" his mother had called. By this time, the four elite Mews had taken Don and Chase away. Bran and Dan had also arrived at the dock.

Perry started to protest. This was something he would be too scared to do on a normal day, but this was Lisa. He was the strongest among them. He was the fastest. He could reach heights they couldn't; he was the perfect bird to go after the evil. Perhaps, if he had two lean mean fire-breathing machines with him; they wouldn't follow anybody except him.

"Go save your sister," Mother had said with a determined and deadly look.

Perry felt his heart spur when he had left with Bran and Dan. His mother hadn't called him to chide him but to encourage him. She believed in him.

Sarah and James also wanted to come. Perry had said no. They would only slow him down.

Now, they were entering Denver after about three hours of flight. They descended until they could make out street signs. Perry could sense that his bones were on the verge of cracking.

They found the house after a while of searching. Their deliberately planned course of action was to circle the house and get a feel for it. It was a farmhouse in the middle of a vast field of crops. Attached to the main house was a small warehouse with high glass windows. He couldn't see through the smudged windows. Apparently, nobody had been in the warehouse for a while, though the main house didn't look abandoned.

As Perry rounded the front for the sixth time, he heard a whimper. It was Lisa's. Perry broke his run, diving straight for the glass windows. Bran yelled that he was diving into a trap, which Perry ignored. The glass shattered on impact. Bound and tied to a pillar of wood, Lisa and Jane knelt on straws. They both looked up when he made his entrance.

Perry transformed.

"No!" Jane yelled. The moment his feet touched the floor, a trap was sprung. The next thing Perry knew, he was being pulled up into an iron net. He struggled with the net to no avail. He glanced at Lisa. She looked at him, her eyes wide with horror. Then, Perry remembered. Lisa didn't yet know about Mews. That was why Jane had yelled. His heart sank. What would happen at her Fall Ritual next summer?

Perry forced the thoughts out of his mind for now; there wouldn't be a Fall Ritual next summer if Lisa was killed. He looked around. Dan and Bran had followed him in and were now hanging from iron nets of their own—nets that were impervious to their fire and metal wings. His brilliant plan was sure going well.

"You shouldn't have come, Perr," muttered Jane with sad eyes. "We were used as baits to lure you here. It's you she wants. But, now she'll kill us all."

A figure stepped out of the shadows and into the light. Perry recognized the scraggly, old one-eyed witch. Hovering in the air behind her were a host of Hubats. Perry's heart began to thump.

The figure pulled a long knife out of her black drabs, leaving Perry to wonder how that was possible. Perry watched the witch approach the girls.

"We know you, Perry," she said in a deadly low voice. "We've seen your heart. We know your fears. You are weak. You are average. And today, you are dead." She pointed the knife at Lisa. Perry's heart skipped a beat. He could feel the cold air blast out of his nostrils.

"She will die first," the woman said. "Then you, boy."

Perry squirmed in the iron net. He screamed and thrashed, reaching for the air. He tried to transform. Nothing.

The woman smiled and approached.

Lisa cringed back at the glinting bade, her chest beginning to heave. "No, no, no," she sobbed, "Please don't."

Jane struggled violently, but her bindings held her tight. Perry had raced across continental America, thinking he was coming to save his sister. He hadn't known that he had raced here to watch her die.

"Hey!" Perry cried. "Don't kill her. It's me you want. Take me!"

The witch paused, looking over to him. "Oh, but we already have you." She took the last step.

Perry glanced at Lisa. She caught his gaze and mouthed: *I love you.* Perry felt his heart tear. Perry shook his head, tears falling down his cheek. The witch raised the knife, her grip on the handle tight, sure, firm. She would not strike twice.

A strong whistle pulsed through the room.

They all looked to the windows from where the Fire Breathers and a red, blue, and white phoenix burst into the room in a shower of shattered glass and a flood of flames. Hubats are really combustible creatures because they incinerated on contact with even a drop of flame. The witch, seeing what had befallen her army, shrilled in frustration. The knife fell from her grip and clattered to the floor as she turned to run, escaping through a side door. Several of the eagles flew in pursuit. The remaining eagles set Perry and his sisters free. The moment Perry's feet were on the ground, he ran to Lisa. They met in the middle. Perry wrapped his arms around her, shutting his eyes.

"I love you back," he said.

They remained there for a moment while the eagles cleaned up the remaining Hubats. Perry knew that he was never leaving her again.

♦ ♦ ♦

That night, his parents and the Fortins arrived in Denver.

The living room of their five-star hotel suite was packed. Mother, Father, Uncle Felix, the buzzard twins, Richard, the Fortins, and the High Lord of the Central Council were present in the spacious apartment. The

High Lord of the Central Council was a tall imperial man with a dark goatee and an air of arrogance around him. He wore an expensive black velvet coat.

Lisa was asleep in the bedroom. When she was up and about, she would want an explanation for what she had seen. Mother had made them promise that they would not utter a word. Lisa's initiation next summer was already in doubt. But, at least she was safe.

The grownups talked about all that had beset the Mews, all of which had surrounded Perry. They had mandated him to be there, yet they had not spoken to him or let him speak. It was not as if he wanted to be there in the first place. He felt weak, tired, and his body ached from head to toe. He just wanted to go to bed. He had defeated the sea monster. The least they could do was let him rest.

"The Crofts have denied affiliation with Don and Chase, Greg," the High Lord said. "There's no need for an all-out provocation."

Greg's eyes burned with intensity. There seemed to be some sort of rivalry between his father and the High Lord. "They attacked my son, tore down my house, and you say we should just sit by?"

"I say you should be smart, Greg," the High Lord replied. "War at a time such as this would be foolhardy. The evil is brewing. We need to be united if we'll survive."

Greg nodded, but he obviously didn't like it.

"Don and Chase were able to escape with the help of a horde of Hubats," Louis Fortin said. His handsome chiseled face was calm. "Only one elite was transferring them to our holding station in Brooklyn. He was jumped. My boys are not yet used to the Hubats attacking in a large number. Our official standing is that the two Crofts are in league with the evil."

The High Lord took a deep breath. He bobbed his head. "There are surely dark times ahead for us. This has never happened before, and it is time we consult with every other council on other continents to let them know what is happening. Greg, I'm going to need you back on the council for this to work."

Greg shook his head. "No, Charles. I'm done with the council."

The man shrugged and stood to his feet. "Consider your stand again, Greg. There are dark times ahead, for both your family and for the Mewranters." The man walked a bit towards the door and stopped by Perry. "There will be those who will seek to take your life, Perry Johnson. But, you have proven yourself a boy of courage and great will. There might be hope in you yet for the Mews to be unified under one rule." Then, he walked out of the room.

The Fortins escorted the High Lord out, while his parents and Uncle Felix escorted the Fortins out. Richard, Jane, and Jake formed a group and chatted excitedly about their near misses with death. Jake, Perry just learned, had escaped their apartment and had kept low at the instruction of their father.

Perry went to the balcony and gazed at the city. The moon was a great big shiny globe in the sky. Two birds flew over to him and perched on the railing. Perry stroked their feathers with his bare hands. They remained silent for a while.

"*We have been summoned back to the White Mountain,*" Bran said. "*It has been an honor fighting alongside you, boss.*"

"*We wish we didn't have to go,*" Dan added.

"I wish you could stay," Perry said, "but you have to go help your people. I have a feeling that I'll be needing your help again sometime soon, anyway."

Perry hugged the birds in turn, and they flapped away, rising into the moon.

Perry stood in the cold wind, listening to the satisfying rhythm of the buzzard twins' and Richard's laughs. His family was happy and whole again. Though many things—hardships—lay ahead of them, questions left unanswered, new facets of himself and his ancestry unveiled, but at least they were a family again. He watched the two large eagles fly away until they were lost beyond the horizon.

"Lisa would be dead if they hadn't helped, you know."

Perry turned to see Uncle Felix standing on the threshold with his hands in his pocket. He looked tired. He joined Perry on the balcony, and they both gazed out at the night.

"Uncle, how did you find us in Denver?" asked Perry.

Uncle Felix chuckled. "Your distress, Perry, is like a blazing fire in the night to the Fire Breathers. When we arrived at the cliff house in Nevada, we found it damaged. A great battle had taken place, and Lisa and Jane were nowhere to be found. We assumed they had been abducted as there was no body lying around for miles in every direction. Then, I and the Fire Breathers who had come with me from the Arctic sensed your distress. It was around that time you were told that Lisa had been kidnapped. I called your mother and she told me what had happened. We immediately began our journey here. Your distress led us to the exact house where you were being held."

Perry thought about this for a second and said, "Thanks for coming, Uncle."

Uncle Felix simply nodded, a gesture that was almost veiled by the darkness. He stood with Perry for a few more minutes before retiring to his bedroom.

Perry stood on the balcony for a while after his uncle had left, thinking about all that had happened since the Fall Ritual. He smiled and then went back into the room to join his siblings' chatter.

ABOUT THE AUTHOR

K achi Ugo is a pharmacist living in Africa. His whole life has revolved around writing. When he was twelve, while his friends still flipped through picture books and comics, he took an interest into thick, picture-less "story books" that opened him up to a whole new world of possibilities and adventures. A decade later, he writes those same books himself. Kachi Ugo is an avid supporter of YA Fantasy. For him, writing is a passion. He relishes the power it gives him to create worlds of his own, where anything and everything is possible.

When he's not writing a novel, he can be found putting up posts at kachiugo.com. Follow him on Instagram @kachiugo3 or on Twitter @KachiUgo.

Morgan James
Speakers Group

We connect Morgan James published
authors with live and online events
and audiences who will benefit
from their expertise.

Morgan James makes all of our titles available
through the Library for All Charity Organization.

www.LibraryForAll.org